SECRET
IN THE
HAYLOFT

Secret In The Hayloft

AND
OTHER STORIES

By Josephine Cunnington Edwards

TEACH Services, Inc.
PUBLISHING
www.TEACHServices.com ▪ (800) 367-1844

Copyright © 2005, 2017 TEACH Services, Inc.
ISBN-13: 978-1-57258-311-5 (Paperback)
Library of Congress Control Number: 2005926211

TEACH Services, Inc.
PUBLISHING
www.TEACHServices.com • (800) 367-1844

DEDICATION

Dedicated to my son Bob,
whose life has been a fulfillment
of all of our dreams for him;
    and to Charles,
whose love and achievements for young people
and things of beauty delighted our hearts;
    and to Alice Princess,
my "little brown baby with sparklin' eyes."

J. C. E.

CONTENTS

SCARS
FOR LIFE

*D*ON'T YOU follow me," the African mother warned her little boy, Yenda-Yenda. "You stay here in the village and play with the other children. Do you remember hearing the leopard crying last night? It is not safe for little boys to be walking in the bush."

"But won't the leopard try to kill you?" asked Yenda-Yenda fearfully.

The mother only laughed comfortingly at her little boy. "See, I am carrying a spear and a knobkerrie, and I am taking Mfiti Khonde, our fierce dog. I will be safe enough. Do not fear."

Yenda-Yenda did not want to stay in the hot village and play. He loved to go with his mother to the garden by the stream when she went to hoe the corn. He could spend his time wading happily, and paddling, and building little dikes in the tiny brook while his mother hoed and watered her cabbages and beans and corn. The days always passed very fast when he could play by the stream.

Even though Yenda-Yenda was very small, he sometimes helped his mother carry water to the young plants. He had a small waterpot that his old grandmother had made especially for him. He could fill it and lift it onto his small woolly head and trot after his mother, back and forth, back and forth. Now today she had told him he couldn't go. He stuck out his bottom lip stubbornly. What foolishness! Mothers were always afraid their children would get hurt. He could see no sense in it at all.

He watched his mother march off with her hoe on her head, carrying her knobkerrie and her spear.

"Come play with us, Yenda-Yenda," cried Musalaboula. "We are playing that we have a store. You and Tiyeni and Kafuno be the customers. You must get some pretty stones to use for money."

For a while Yenda-Yenda amused himself by pretending that the big flat banana leaves were bright pieces of cloth, that sand was salt, and red dirt was sugar. The boys had some little pots of water, which Musalaboula declared was peanut oil.

But the sun glared down upon Yenda-Yenda's small head, and every once in a while a trickle of sweat ran down his small back, making it itch. While he was scratching in the hard, baked soil for a small red stone with which to buy some "peanut oil," he suddenly thought of the garden by the stream. He stopped digging, his dusty hands hanging limply over his knees as he stood there in the scorching sun.

"The grass is wet and cool, and the stream is full to the brink down there," he whispered to himself, looking off down the bush path. "I could put my whole face down in the water to quench the fierce thirst I feel right now."

"Come on, Yenda-Yenda! Let us go and buy!" cried Tiyeni. "Let us buy everything Musalaboula has."

"I can't play now," he told his friends, for he had given in to the lush and lovely dream of the cool waterside and his mother's hoe going "ponk, ponk, ponk" near at hand.

"I can go quickly," he whispered to himself. "And though she might beat me with a stick, it wouldn't hurt for long."

All at once Yenda-Yenda knew he was going to disobey his mother. He felt a little scared, for mother could beat hard if she got angry. But before he had time to think again, he found himself running very fast toward the garden. He heard the boys shouting faintly in the village as he ran deeper into the cool reaches of the forest. Only a little farther, and he would see the tassels of the corn, and the yellow pumpkins. He was running very fast now, but not so fast that he didn't hear a crash in the tough bushes nearby.

Suddenly a huge tawny form leaped toward him. He stopped short and let out a terrible scream: "The leopard!"

The first leap went clear over Yenda-Yenda's head, and the great cat turned to see where the small boy had disappeared. Yenda-Yenda caught one glimpse of her as she sat hunched low, her giant hindquarters rocking, ready for another leap.

"Mother! Mother! Mother!"

His shrieks filled the whole forest. Then suddenly the sky and the earth, the mountains and the trees, seemed to split right open as the big leopard landed, crushing Yenda-Yenda violently to the earth.

But the dog and the mother had heard. No sooner had the leopard landed on Yenda-Yenda than the brave little dog was there, too. He seized the back flank of the beast and bit and tore viciously, while mother swung the knobkerrie.

While the awful fight went on, Yenda-Yenda lay unconscious. The leopard had torn away a large piece of his scalp and part of his ear with her cruel claws.

God must have been with the brave African mother, for she succeeded in killing the leopard.

It took Yenda-Yenda a long time to get well, but he finally did. He is a man now. When he talks to his own boys and girls about obeying, he shows them his scars. All over the back of his head very little hair is growing.

"That's because I didn't learn to obey my mother," he tells them; and they trace the thick, ridgy scars with their fingers and promise they will always be obedient.

THE EGG-MONEY BOOK, PART I

*T*HE GATE didn't quite swing shut when she came into the garden. A piece of rope weighted down with a leaky old teapot full of stones usually pulled it into place, but the upper hinge had come loose, and it had been dragging a little lately. She shook her faded, drab apron at a jabbering old rooster who was conducting two of his hen friends toward a choice meal in the new lettuce bed. They protestingly made their exit before her threatening onslaught, and she patiently closed the gate.

Muriel's thoughts were always two jumps ahead of her busy hands. While she was filling the deep, flat tin pan with the tiny new lettuce leaves the size of cats' ears, she made her plans for the day's work ahead of her. She must churn and get the butter into molds and down to the cool springhouse. She must make some cherry pies. Henry had picked the cherries before breakfast from the sprawling, gnarled old Montmorency tree in the yard. Then her truant mind began to wander down forbidden paths. She felt like Maude Muller, dreaming with an ache in her heart of what she might have been.

A year ago she had been at Calhoun Teachers' College. She had been proud of being on the honor roll every six weeks when the grades were posted. In just one more year she would graduate. Oh, the joy of it!

Even now, her lip trembled at the thought, and she felt that if she cried for a hundred years, she would still be miserably unhappy.

Just six weeks before the end of her junior year it had happened. She never forgot the terrible sensation she experienced when she was called down to the dean's office to face a messenger boy. She remembered then how her heart had plunged with a horrible fear. With trembling fingers she had torn open the ominous yellow envelope. The letters swam before her eyes.

"Mother has had a stroke. Come home immediately.
                                                        "Father"

Oh, the agony of packing and leaving school! She was falling apart inside. She worried constantly over her mother and longed to be with her, but at the same time she grieved over her schoolwork.

Now the early spring grass was growing on mother's grave, and Muriel had taken over keeping house for father and the boys. Her college days were finished; she was sure of that. With a tremulous little sigh she rose from her knees, shook the fine little scattering of powdery earth from her skirts, and started up the garden path. There was dirt under her fingernails. She felt unkempt and miserable. Involuntarily she stooped down and pulled up a ragweed that was getting a start by the gate and threw it over to the chickens. Then, latching the gate carefully, she turned down the little path around the white lilac bush. Suddenly she came face to face with a strange young man. The meeting surprised both of them. He had seen her in the garden, but he hadn't seen her leave because she was hidden by the high perennial shrubs that bordered the fence. They stood for an instant, the two of them, each sizing up the other.

Then the young man smiled. "Good morning. May I help you with your vegetables?" Reaching, he took them from her hands, stepped aside, and let her precede him to the kitchen door. She put a newspaper down on the workbench, and he set the pan of vegetables on it. Then he brushed his hands lightly together and smiled again. Stooping, he took a book from his briefcase.

"My name is Moore," he said, "Stephen Moore. I'm selling religious books to earn a scholarship to college. May I show you what I have?" And he brought out a small black leather volume lettered in gold leaf.

"*The Great Controversy Between Christ and Satan,*" Muriel read from the cover. The young Mr. Moore began to explain the book to her in his smooth, low voice. He told her about the destruction of Jerusalem, about the apostles and missionaries, reformers and martyrs, as his fingers slowly turned the pages for her. The picture of Wycliffe sitting up in his bed rebuking the friars was impressive. She looked twice at the pictures of the martyrs.

Muriel listened eagerly. She had been working on a major in history at Calhoun, and she knew this must be a wonderful book. But what was the young man saying now? Something about signs of the times and the Lord coming soon. What did it all mean? She had to know. She could pay for the book out of the egg money father had said could be hers. So before she began fixing her vegetables for dinner, she signed her name to the order blank, and the literature evangelist started to say good-bye and express his thanks.

"Wait just a minute!" exclaimed the girl on a sudden impulse. "Why don't you stay and eat dinner with us? It will be noon before you can reach the next farmhouse. I'd like for my father and brothers to see that book."

She showed him the washroom which the men used for cleaning up. There was a sink, piped so that the waste water flowed down a slope to the hen yard, where it made a regular muddy Utopia for the ducks and geese. The pitcher pump brought up quantities of clean rainwater. Stephen Moore filled the brightly scoured washpan full and washed the sweat and dust from his hands and face. He was grateful for the hospitality. Wouldn't it be wonderful if he could find a place like this where he could make his headquarters? It was in the very heart of his territory. He could use a bicycle and work out from here like spokes on a buggy wheel. He would pray about it, and the Lord would show him the best way.

Then he went into the quaint, old-fashioned parlor, where he had been asked to wait until dinner was ready. The old tufted leather sofa looked so inviting that he could not resist the temptation to lie down. The road had been so hot! His feet throbbed. A breeze came in through the open window, and the clean muslin curtains moved lazily back and forth over the brown sill. It looked homelike—the green Axminster rug with its elaborate old-fashioned pattern of scrolls and curlicues; the brown oatmeal paper, and pictures of Rachel at the well and of Baby Stuart, on the wall. A clean glass vase full of trembling striped grasses stood on the organ. It was peaceful here. If only . . . but suddenly Stephen Moore, warm and exhausted, was asleep on a strange sofa in a strange house.

In the kitchen Muriel watched the clock with anxious eyes. She almost forgot the stranger in the rush of last-minute things to do as she hurried from the stove to the sink, from the sink to the dining room, and back to the stove again.

When both hands of the clock were pointing straight up, Muriel wearily started serving the soup. Then she heard the voices of the men, coming up from the field for dinner. Hurriedly she put the chairs in place and ran out to lay clean towels and washcloths in the washroom. She was gratified to see that the "book agent" had rinsed out the washpan and hung his towel and washcloth on the rack. Then she went in to set the hot foods on the table.

2

There were new green beans seasoned with country butter. There were scalloped potatoes, crusty and aromatic in their deep brown baking dish. She had fixed the lettuce with scrambled eggs, the way her father liked it. The cherry pies, oozing thick red juice, stood fresh and ready to cut on the pantry shelf. When she had brought in the huge plate of biscuits and the bowl of gravy, she went to call the stranger. The noise of the men talking had wakened him, and he was sitting up when she entered the room.

She made the necessary introductions to her father and the boys, and they all gathered around the table. The talk went pleasantly enough until they were eating their pie. Then father turned suddenly and said, "What was the name of that book you're selling?"

Muriel never forgot the look on her father's face. There was an element of sudden suspicion darkening his eyes. The young salesman looked straight at his host when he answered, *"The Great Controversy."* Muriel saw her father's eyes narrow and harden, his lips straighten out into thin lines. She held her breath.

Father was fairly spluttering. "Why, why—ain't that a Seventh-day Adventist book?" he queried, his sharp voice rising to a thin rasp.

"Yes, it is," said the young man calmly. "I'm a Seventh-day Adventist myself. I'm planning to go to college and be a minister."

By this time father was fairly choking with wrath. Muriel looked at him with amazement.

"Then we don't want it!" he shrilled. "I won't have my children reading doctrines of devils. Keepin' Saturday for Sunday. Preachin' the end of the world! You just mark our name off'n that order blank, Muriel, and double quick. You hear me?"

The blood rushed to Muriel's face. Her dander was up. She was working hard. She was twenty-two years old. She was buying the book with her own egg money. Surely, twelve hours a day in the kitchen, the yard, the garden, and the dairy gave her *some* rights.

"Father," she said in a low, even voice, "I ordered that book. I'll pay for it myself. I want it. There is no 'doctrine of devils,' as you say, in it. It's all history and Bible. Don't be so narrow-minded."

The angry man said nothing more, but he wouldn't speak to or look at the young stranger again. He got up, shoved his chair back angrily, and strode out. Muriel could have cried with embarrassment. Her brothers were kinder. They shook hands with Mr. Moore, and Henry even asked him to "excuse Pop for kickin' up a fuss. His bark is worse than his bite. He's always been that way. Thinks everyone's goin' to hell except those in his own church."

Having gotten through this unusually long speech, big, kind Henry got his straw hat from the nail by the door and went out. Stephen Moore had gotten up from the table and was looking at Muriel. When she raised her head, he smiled.

"Don't feel bad about me," he said. "I've learned to

take things like this with a smile. Are you sure you still want the book?"

She had to cry a little then to relieve her jangled nerves.

"Yes, I do," she answered tremulously. "I want it worse than ever now. I love my father, but he is as narrow and bigoted as a Pharisee. I'm going to pay you in full for it, right now. You can send it to me by mail. I don't imagine you'll want to come back and deliver it."

"No," replied Stephen, "I won't mail it. I want to come back."

THE EGG-MONEY BOOK, PART II

*H*ARVEST WAS in full swing when Stephen Moore started making his deliveries. He had rented an asthmatic old car and piled the back seat full of books. He knew he would earn his scholarship this summer and more. It would be an easier senior year at college than he had expected. He could join the Glee Club and take that extra class in expression. He could have time for Seminar and Men's Club instead of going out at three thirty in the morning to milk the cows. He whistled a happy little tune while he parked his car and studied the road map.

The next place on his list was the farm where that brave girl bought the book against her father's orders. She surely seemed nice. Well educated—you could tell by the way she talked. And she was pretty, too.

21

Muriel met him at the front door. She had been watching for him, for he had sent her a card early in the week, notifying her of the delivery day.

"I'm so glad to get the book," she said. "I've thought a great deal on what you said about the Lord's coming. I've been looking it up in the Bible. I believe it, too. Why, it couldn't be any other way!"

Stephen stood and smiled at her, twirling his hat. "Of course not," he agreed. "There's not another doctrine in the Bible that is more obvious. Every book in the New Testament teaches it."

"Won't you sit down a minute?" Muriel asked him. "There's another thing I want to tell you. Do you remember how father accused you of keeping Saturday for Sunday? Well, that made me curious. My Aunt Hetty left several religious books here when she died, and I went up in the attic and found a wonderful one that explains what the Bible says about nearly every subject that you can think of."

She went over to the bookcase and brought out a dilapidated copy of *Bible Readings for the Home Circle.* "Did you ever see a book like this?" she asked.

For an answer he opened his briefcase and showed her his own copy, bound in red leather. "Indeed I have," he assured her, laughing. "I wouldn't be without it."

"Well," she continued, "father made me curious. I decided to find out what this Saturday business meant. And I've found out! The seventh day truly is the Sabbath. Do you keep Saturday?"

Stephen was amazed beyond belief. This intelligent young woman had virtually read herself into the Seventh-day Adventist Church in six weeks! It was unbelievable.

Then he assured her that he kept the Bible Sabbath. His lifework would be to bring people to Christ. That was why he was going to a missionary college. That was why he was selling these books. *The Great Controversy* alone had brought many people to Christ. He was doing double duty by distributing good books and preparing himself for the gospel ministry at the same time.

Muriel was deeply impressed. Then she told him that she, too, loved going to school, that she had only a year of college work to finish when mother died and she had been called home to take care of the family.

They had prayer together. Muriel looked sweet and childlike kneeling there by the old Sleepy Hollow chair. The tears dropped through her fingers onto the faded green plush as she prayed her short, halting petition.

When they arose, she told him that she was going to keep the Bible Sabbath. "I don't know whether father will even let me stay here," she said bravely. But one look into her earnest brown eyes told him that she would do it anyway. Stephen left his card and asked Muriel to get in touch with him if she had trouble. He promised to write to her and send her literature that would bring her more information about the Bible.

Her first letter came while he was packing his trunk to go to college. It was a courageous little note, and he could read her fine determination between the lines.

"Father raised a terrible fuss at first," she told him. "He raved and he roared and he yelled, until people passing by on the road craned their necks to look. I didn't say a word, but he kept right on. It was really awful. The more he scolded, the more determined I was. He couldn't move me. Pray for me, though. I need fortitude."

Quickly Stephen wrote an encouraging reply. Then he subscribed to *Present Truth* and sent it to her. He could hardly keep her situation off his mind. He had seen her only twice, but he could picture her going busily about her immaculate kitchen, her neat garden, or working among her old-fashioned flowers.

Later in September a letter came from her that crystallized an idea for Stephen. Muriel should come to college. She was intelligent, and he knew she could be a successful worker for God. Muriel's letter had been short, and it was full of heartbreak.

"Father says I must go—says I can't stay at home and keep the Sabbath. He has already engaged a woman named Lyddy Myers to keep house for him. I don't know where I'll go. I have some money of my own which my mother left me. Friday is my last day at home. It nearly breaks my heart. But I won't give up. I must follow my Saviour. I read in the Bible that if father and mother forsake me, then the Lord will take me up, so I'll put my trust in Him."

Stephen finished the letter and raced directly across the campus to tell the whole story to the business manager.

The result was that Muriel went to college. The first Friday evening, when the bell announced to the little community that Sabbath had begun, she thought she was in heaven. Everything was perfect. She feasted her eyes, her ears, her soul.

She registered as a senior—in the same class with Stephen Moore, and the year was gone almost before it started. Deep in her womanly heart she knew there could never be anyone as wonderful as Stephen. He had brought her the wonderful gospel message, and he seemed to her to be the ideal man. Occasionally at certain gatherings where the young people chose partners, Stephen sought her out. But that meant nothing, of course. He knew that she was a stranger, and he wanted to help her get acquainted. Sometimes she saw him striding across the campus or in the library, his head bent over a book. He always had a friendly greeting for her, and she was always pleased to meet him anywhere.

Muriel entered enthusiastically into the extracurricular activities. She went with the Sunshine Band to hold meetings in the local jail. She sang at the church meetings near the college, in towns like Decatur, Glenwood, Paw Paw, and Benton Harbor. She addressed envelopes for the literature band. She made A's and B's in all her classes. Then graduation came at last, and Muriel had her B.A. degree.

Two days after graduation, when she was wondering what she would do next, the dean of women came up to her room to tell her that Mr. Moore was waiting to see her in the parlor.

Stephen was looking out the window toward the old woodshop building when she came in. She couldn't keep her heart from thumping. Surely he would hear it! Oh, wasn't he handsome! Wasn't he tall! Then a kind of sadness seized her. Surely such happiness could never be meant for her. He was too busy to think about girls.

Stephen turned and pulled up a chair for her and another for himself. "Muriel," he said softly, "I hesitate to ask you—I'm afraid you'll think I'm taking advantage of you. I've fought this feeling all year. There are so many people who could offer you more than I can—but, Muriel, I must tell you. I love you. Will you marry me? Then we can go into God's work together. Do you care for me just a little bit, Muriel?"

But Muriel couldn't answer. She caught her breath in sheer astonishment and lifted her honest brown eyes to look at him. He read the truth in them and laughed softly. Then, taking her hand in his, he told her that he had a call to connect with a conference in the South as a ministerial intern. There wouldn't be much money in it at first, but they would have youth, love, and an important job that would consume all their interests and energies.

"And we'll have our books," added Muriel enthusiastically. "Our schoolbooks, and my egg-money book."

"Oh, yes, that egg-money book!" Stephen repeated softly. "I got a scholarship and a wife last summer!"

"And I got a wonderful husband and a chance to work for God, and I owe it all to the egg-money book!" Muriel replied.

SECRET IN
THE HAYLOFT

*J*OHNNY crept into the backyard, looked all around to see that no one was watching, then vanished into the shed, where the fireplace logs were stacked neatly along the wall. Cleats nailed to the wall led up to a hayloft, where father now kept spare things such as a bundle of shingles, a keg half full of nails, a neat pile of lath, and some boards.

Johnny had a guilty look on his face. He stood up as straight as he could under the low, slanting ceiling, and pulled a half-empty package of cigarettes out of his pants pocket. He turned the pocket inside out, to be sure no shreds of tobacco had stuck to it, and brushed it industriously. Then he went to the eaves, pushed a loose board aside, and hid the package.

"A guy's got to be free!" He pushed his bottom lip out stubbornly. "I'm a person myself. I don't like for folks to be telling me all the time what I can do and what I can't do."

He climbed down the ladder and started across the woodshed toward the door.

"Johnny!" mother called from the porch. "Are you out there? I didn't hear you come in. I've got some orange juice fixed for you."

A flush of shame crept across Johnny's face. While he'd been sneaking cigarettes into the woodshed, mother had been doing something special for him, remembering how a boy feels when he's thirsty.

"I'm here, Mother," he called. "I'm getting some wood for the fireplace." He had to explain his being in the woodshed someway. Mother must never find out what he'd really been doing.

He turned, his heart and face burning, and picked up three large logs, being careful not to snag his jacket on the bark. His new navy blue jacket was so much nicer than the ragged old stretched and discolored sweater his buddy Phil had been wearing that afternoon. There was a hole in Phil's pants leg, too, where his knee showed right through.

Johnny was worried for fear mother might smell the cigarette he had smoked earlier that afternoon in Phil's dirty kitchen. But he had smoked only one, and Phil had given him some cloves to chew on.

"That'll take it off yer breath," Phil had said. He sneered as he shook the cloves out of a dingy tin can he had taken from the untidy cupboard. "Boy, I feel sorry for you. You're just like a jailbird, and yer pop and mom are the jailers."

Johnny hadn't said a word. He was angry, for that just wasn't true, and he knew it. No one in his family had ever even been close to a jail. But poor Phil was well acquainted with jails, laws, cops, courts, and judges. He had explained those things proudly to the boys at school. And he whispered to Johnny, "Well, pop got caught again. Believe me, when I get bigger, I ain't gonna get caught as easy as he does. He don't use his head. Me, I'm gonna be smarter than him."

While Phil was making fun of Johnny and his "jailers," Johnny had taken a curious look around Phil's house. He had never been there before, and it was horrible.

The kitchen, where the boys sat, was ugly and dark. It smelled of food that should have been thrown out long before. Rotting potatoes, stale bread, and a dozen other ugly smells irritated Johnny's sensitive nose. Light struggled through a flyspecked broken window on one side of the room. Sometime in the past, the things that hung from a string stretched across two nails might have been curtains, but they didn't look like curtains now. The floor was caked with dirt. The table and the iron sink were piled with dirty dishes. There was a cold, rusty stove, with ashes spilling out of a broken place in the side.

From where he sat, Johnny could see the front room and the bedroom. The whole shack looked to him like a tornado of disorder.

"He's got his nerve, feeling sorry for me," Johnny thought, remembering his neat, well-ordered home.

Johnny had given Phil a quarter for the pack of cigarettes and a small box of matches.

"I'll give you half of the cigarettes if you get them for me," Johnny bargained generously. Phil grabbed the half pack with gleaming eyes and experienced fingers. Then he had stood and watched Johnny try his first cigarette. He told him how to hold it and what to do once he got it burning. Phil was experienced, and he was delighted to see how quickly Johnny got the hang of it.

"When you get used to them cigarettes," he said, "you'll like them better than food when you're hungry. I like one as soon as I get through eating, same as pop and mom. They learned me to like them."

Johnny rinsed out his mouth at the filthy kitchen sink. He felt terrible as he walked out onto the broken porch, told Phil good-bye, and started home. He sneaked around the back way so that he could hide the cigarettes in the woodshed before he went into the house.

When he carried the logs through the kitchen, his mother was tying on a bright flowered apron over her good dress. She smiled.

"Thanks, Johnny, for building us a fire. It's a chilly evening, and it'll be nice to have the house warm and cheerful when dad comes home." Mother's voice was gentle and sweet.

The kitchen was bright, and the soup was bubbling on the stove. The table was set neatly. Potato soup, hot cornbread, sliced tomatoes, and pumpkin pie! What a difference from Phil's house with its cracked plates smeared with old egg and gravy.

Johnny got the fire started in the living-room fireplace, and it was soon crackling and making flickering shadows on the walls. He looked down the hallway. He knew that the bed in his room would be clean and that his room was full of books and clean clothes—and comfort. The model airplane dad had helped him make was hanging from the ceiling, and a big model ship stood on a shelf above the dresser. The bathroom was gleaming pink tile. He thought briefly of Phil's smelly iron sink.

"Poor Phil," he whispered. "He probably never saw a house like this one. Dad isn't a jailer. He's good to me. And mother wouldn't think of running away. I think she'd love me even if she knew I had those cigarettes out in the woodshed."

He went to the bathroom to wash his hands before dinner. He brushed his teeth again as an added precaution. "Boy, I don't want them to smell it."

Just one year before this the Hargen family had become Seventh-day Adventists. How that had happened was an interesting story in itself. Strange letters started coming from dad's brother, who was out West in the navy. Something had happened to Uncle Jim that had puzzled the whole family. He had taken up with a new religion, one that seemed very strange to Mr. and Mrs. Hargen.

"I think it's a good thing for Jim to belong to a church," dad said. "But I hate to see anyone take anything as seriously as Jim is taking this new religion. It must be because of that accident he had."

"How could that be?" mother asked.

Dad said, "He went to a sanitarium that is owned by the church he has joined. I think they took advantage of his being so badly hurt."

"That's his way of showing gratitude!" Mother poured dad some more hot coffee and refilled the sugar bowl. She sat down at the table with him.

Dad shook his head. "Jim says that's not it. I wrote and asked him point-blank. He says it's as plain as the nose on your face, and he was surprised he hadn't realized it before. And besides that, he wound up marrying one of the nurses from the hospital!"

Jim came to visit soon after that, so that the family could meet his new wife, Brenda. The moment she arrived, she walked right into everyone's heart. Jim just stood around adoring her, smiling all the time.

Mother and dad were nervous and a little stiff at first, but that was over before an hour had passed. In the first place, Brenda was interesting to talk to. Her folks had been missionaries to the South Sea Islands, and the stories she had to tell fascinated everyone.

"I'll tell you," dad said to mother after they had gone to their bedroom that night, "that sweet girl and Jim are so deluded. I'm going to get her talking, and maybe we can make them see that they're both clear out of step with the rest of the world."

"Take it easy!" Mother was bustling around folding

the bedspread. "She isn't exactly ignorant. She has a college education, and her father's a minister."

"Won't do any harm to try," father said. "At least I can find out where they got some of those notions."

The very next day dad began to question Brenda, and to his amazement, Jim was delighted. "You won't get that wife of mine in a corner," he said, laughing.

Sure enough, Brenda answered every question dad asked her with a text from the Bible.

The first thing the Hargen family knew, they were studying the Bible every night with Brenda and Jim. The young couple made it so interesting with stories and historic happenings that even Johnny listened.

Mother hurried them through supper so that they could get together in the parlor to hear what Brenda had to say next.

"She's as good as a preacher," dad whispered to mother one evening.

"Better," she whispered back.

Then suddenly it seemed as if all the things they had thought were true and reliable were crumbling away.

"I had no idea the Bible had so much in it," dad said one night. "I declare, it's almost bewildering to see that pretty young woman flipping the pages of the Bible, reading here and there and everywhere, proving her point like a college professor or something."

Mother said, "Brenda says the Adventist Church has what they call church schools, where the Bible is taught to the children every day. I wish we could get Johnny into a school like that. It would surely be a good thing for him. He's right at the age now where he's picking up ideas I don't like."

"Maybe we can," dad answered.

From the time of Jim and Brenda's visit, the entire life of the Hargen family had changed. Even the food on the table was different. Before they went back to California, Brenda gave mother several cooking lessons, and in the place of meat they now had some delicious dishes called roasts. And because Johnny told Brenda he was surely going to miss hamburgers, she took him into the kitchen and taught him how to make something that she called burgers.

"Mom, taste them," he had said as he carried the platter to the supper table. "Aunt Brenda is toasting the buns and slicing the onions. But I made the burgers. Whenever we want burgers, just you ask me."

He stuck his recipe in his own handwriting to the side of the refrigerator with Scotch tape so that he would have it handy:

"1 cup cooked oatmeal 1 teaspoon salt
 1 peeled raw potato, grated 1 pinch sage
 4 teaspoons oil 1 teaspoon Savita or Sovex
 ½ cup ground walnuts 1 teaspoon flour
 1 cup toast crumbs Enough milk to moisten

"Make into patties, and fry brown."

For a while Johnny wanted burgers every day; but mother learned so many other things Johnny liked that he was soon down to once a week.

There were some other things about his family's new religion Johnny didn't like quite that much. He loved to go to the ball games on Friday night and to the show on Saturday afternoon. Sometimes dad had gone with him to the ball game, and occasionally mother had gone with him to the show. But they didn't go anymore.

School was different, too. Mother and dad took Johnny out of public school and sent him to the local Adventist church school. It was out in the country a little way, and there was a big playground. There were three teachers in the school, and Johnny liked a lot of things about it.

But he had his unhappy moments. He had to break off with his friends from public school and not run around with them as he once did.

"A guy can't have a bit of fun anymore," he growled when dad explained one night about choosing good music on the radio, and why some television shows are better than others.

"There are some good shows, Johnny, and we'll study the *TV Guide*, and decide. But too many TV programs make children mentally lazy. We have lots of good books to read, and I think TV is making a whole generation of children who don't read nearly enough."

Johnny's face was sullen. "What can a guy do?" he demanded. "It's 'Don't do this' and 'Don't do that' all the time. I wish Aunt Brenda and Uncle Jim had never come."

Dad got up and went with Johnny into his bedroom. They were in there a long time. Dad talked very kindly to him and told him he understood why boys feel rebellious sometimes, but he was not going to allow him to act hateful around home.

"There are some things a boy must not say to older people, and I have noticed that you are getting a little impudent, Johnny. I won't have it, and you'll be punished if you talk that way again. Mother and I are glad we have found the Adventist Church, for it will mean the kingdom of heaven for all of us if we are faithful. We have learned a better way of life, and I want you to be as thankful for it as we are."

Johnny still scowled a little, though he was ashamed of himself, for dad had been good to him.

"But the boys at the Garfield School—whenever I go past them, Dad, they laugh and make fun of me. They call me names." He stammered the last, avoiding his father's eyes. How could he explain Phil's yell of laughter when he heard that Johnny was going to church school?

"Get a load of this, you guys!" Phil had shouted. "Old Johnny's goin' to a church school. He's goin' to learn to be a deacon." A shout of derisive laughter followed Johnny that day as he hurried off down the street, ashamed and angry.

Dad put his arm around Johnny.

"Be a good soldier, son. This is your battle. I have my battles—Aunt Myra and grandma are on my neck. Mother is having her trials, too. At the office some of the men laugh at me, but I don't care. It's worth it."

Reluctantly, and only half-convinced, Johnny got up and went to do his chores. He tried to avoid his old friends when he had to go to the store or on an errand uptown, but he was not always successful. Down inside he wished he could still fool around with the boys from his old school. He didn't tell his father, but he went to a poolroom several times, just to watch the boys shoot the balls. The devil kept right after Johnny.

This state of affairs continued until after Christmas. One day after Johnny got home from school, he went out to ride on his bicycle. Mother was gone to the Dorcas meeting, and he was alone. He met Phil Beavers, one of the boys from the school, who had made life particularly miserable for him. They had been pretty good friends before, though mother and dad didn't approve of him.

"Hi there, Deacon," Phil shouted gaily. "How's all that holy stuff comin' along?"

Johnny clenched his fists and looked angrily at the ill-clad, shabby boy. He remembered many times when he had paid Phil's way to movies and ball games. He had felt very superior and good, back in those days, helping Phil out.

Phil saw Johnny's angry look and stopped laughing.

"Aw, don't get mad," Phil said, coming close. "I ain't forgot you was always good to me. You bought me hamburgers and Cokes more than any of the other boys. I just miss you, that's all, and I feel sorry for you. You ain't having no fun at all, the guys say."

"Well, quit calling me Deacon, if you haven't forgotten." Johnny wished he had the nerve to punch Phil right in the nose. "I've never done anything mean to you. It's not my fault that my folks have joined another church."

"Aw, I know it. My old man makes me do things I don't wanna do lotsa times. I know how ya feel. Boy, look! He gimme this black eye last night, just for nothin'."

Phil's left eye was pitifully swollen. Purple and green streaks ran down his cheeks and onto his pinched nose.

"What did you do?"

"Well, I——" Phil looked around to see that no one was near. He whispered, "I told the boys I ran into a door in the dark. I don't want them to know dad beats me up all the time.

"Johnny, don't tell on me. But I took his pack of cigarettes an' a dollar of his money while he was layin' there drunk. Boy, I had to do somethin'. I hadn't et in two days, and when I got the money, I et five hamburgers. When he woke up, he knew I done it, and he nearly killed me. But, Johnny, he did look funny, when he was comin' out, pawin' all over the floor for his cigarettes. I busted out laughin', and boy, did he light into me!" Phil indulged in a shrill laugh, and slapped his dirty trousers.

"Where's your mom, Phil?" Johnny asked.

"Mom lit out and left us a month ago. But it ain't much better when she's there. She hits hard, too; and she gets as drunk as pop. She'll come back, though. She always does."

Johnny looked mystified.

"Lit out?" he asked. "What do you mean? Don't mothers—I mean, aren't mothers supposed to stay at home and cook and wash and take care of——"

He got no further. Phil's laugh sounded louder than ever, though there was nothing funny in it. He reached up and touched his sore eye carefully, for it hurt.

"Ain't you the green one! Mothers like *mine* go and come when they want. And so do I. I ain't in jail like you are, Johnny."

The devil was whispering to Johnny that day. He made Johnny forget his dresser drawers full of clean clothes and the kitchen that always smelled of good food. He forgot about his dad, who had never been cruel to him in his life.

When Phil kept on teasing him, Johnny took a quarter out of his pocket and asked Phil if he would mind getting him a pack of cigarettes. He was amazed at himself, for he knew cigarettes were bad for him. Brenda had told about how serious lung cancer can be. But the old devil kept telling him he was not having one bit of fun and there wasn't anything like a cigarette to turn a boy into a man.

"That's more like it," Phil shouted. "You're good old Johnny again. I'll go right now and get 'em for you, and you can have a little fun at least."

"Here, get a hamburger, too," Johnny said, giving him more money. "You might be hungry."

"I am," Phil admitted. "There ain't a thing to eat in the house, and pop's gone somewhere, I don't know where. Boy, thanks! I am hungry." And he was gone.

When Johnny hid the cigarettes in the loft above the woodshed, he promised himself he would smoke only that one pack. He didn't see Phil for several days.

A few nights later, Johnny made the best burgers they had ever had.

"These taste wonderful, Johnny." Dad put one in a big whole-wheat bun mother had made that afternoon. "Pass the onions, Mother."

Johnny thought of Phil and his miserable home, and of the days he went hungry and cold. If he could sit here at the table and eat and have good folks like mother and dad—Johnny thought of the cigarettes hidden in the wood-house loft. He almost choked, he felt so terrible. All of a sudden he burst out crying, harder than he had cried for a long time.

"Why, son!" Father jumped up and came around to him. "Are you sick? What's the matter?"

It didn't take long for the story to get out between sobs. No one said a word for a few minutes.

"That poor boy," mother said. "I wonder if we couldn't get him. He certainly isn't getting any care at home."

"Oh, would you? Would you?" Johnny cried, hardly able to believe his ears.

"Do you think he'd give us trouble if we took him?" mother asked. "He might have some habits he wouldn't want to break."

"Mother, if Phil had a home like this, he'd think he was in heaven. His place is awful. And his mom and pop both are gone now. He told me so today."

"And he is there all alone?" mother asked.

"Yes. And you ought to see his eye, where his pop hit him."

That evening, while mother did the dishes, dad and Johnny went over to the shack by the river where poor Phil lived. A feeble lamp flickered through the flyspecked windowpane. When they knocked at the door, Phil opened it just a crack. They saw that he had been crying.

They took Phil home that night for a visit, until dad and mother could decide what to do and make up their minds if it would work out. A bath, a haircut, and some of Johnny's clothes made him a different boy. Mother put a poultice on his swollen eye. And she fed him a good hot supper as soon as he was cleaned up.

Johnny watched him eating soup and potatoes and polishing off his burger. "We call those things burgers," he said. "And I made them myself."

"You didn't!" Phil scoffed.

"I did too! Didn't I, Mother?"

"You surely did. Do you like them, Phil?"

"Best things I ever ate. Do you think I could learn to make them?"

"I'll teach you," Johnny promised.

In the months that followed, dad and mother grew to love Phil so much that they got permission to keep him, and soon he began to learn what love really means. He learned how wonderful Jesus is. He learned to love church school, and he and Johnny had a great time going to school and playing together. And he did learn to make the burgers, too.

ONE LOST DRESS

*T*HIS ALL happened when I was a fat, squalling baby in a dress so long that it took five yards of material to make it. I have heard the story told so often that it almost seems as if I remember watching it happen, but of course I don't.

My father had a grocery store on Fifth Street. The store was in a long room in the front of the building, and the house was built right onto the back. When dinner was ready, daddy could walk right from the store into the house. There was a yard at the back where my brothers and sisters could play away from the street. My mother thought the street was dangerous, with all the big horses and wagons going by.

One day my older brother, Willie, came running in, his curly head wagging with excitement.

"Mother! Ethel! Charlie! Mary! There's a thing—a thing runnin' without nothin' pullin' it! Runnin' all by itself up on Willard Street. You never saw the likes of it! It's runnin' with its own insides, someway, and it's smokin' and smellin' and——"

Well, they all ran up to Willard Street, and there, sure enough, was one of the Ketzelman men in a brand-new horseless carriage. He had on goggles and a cap and was steering straight down the middle of the bumpy street. Men stood off to one side, holding the heads of their scared horses, and women on the sidewalk clutched tightly to their children's hands, telling them not to dare go near the thing, for it was sure to explode.

That night the family talked all during supper about the strange new invention.

"Those horseless carriages will *never* be of any general use," my father prophesied. "They're too dangerous. Women would never want to drive them. You don't raise gasoline the way you can raise oats for horses. And the cost is too great for an ordinary family to pay. Only hotheads will be driving those things, for I hear that gasoline is very explosive."

Mother agreed with him. It wouldn't be long before folks would forget about horseless carriages.

The family stopped talking about buggies that ran by themselves, for a much more exciting thing was happening. A brand-new Adventist church was being built, and everyone had gotten pretty excited about it.

That summer there had been a camp meeting in the

town. So many folks were baptized that they had orga-
nized a church. Since there was no church building, the
members had rented a store and met there for a while.
Then they rented a house and used the front room for their
church auditorium. Now they were to have a fine new
church all their own, and everyone was excited about it.
Each member was trying to do something to raise money.
Even the children put pennies in the building fund.

Every night or two, father and mother and the children
would walk down Madison Street to Ninth Street, then
up Ninth three blocks to watch the church building grow.
It was hard to wait, for the new church was going to be
wonderful. A long room in the front would be used as a
school, and the teacher had already been hired for the
coming school year. Ethel and Billy and Charlie would go
to school there.

That night, while Ethel did the dishes, mother turned
down the beds and put the baby and Chet and little Mary
to bed. Ethel, being the oldest, was allowed to stay up a
little later, and she sat by the table in the dining room
listening while daddy and Pastor Stone talked about plans
for the new church. They were sitting in the living room,
but she could hear every word they said if she sat very still.
The plans thrilled the little girl. Ethel was twelve going
on thirteen, and thought she was not so little after all. She
could bake bread by herself now, and this summer mother
had let her make pies twice. Mother said there was no one
better to take care of the children, and that she felt as
safe with them in Ethel's hands as if Ethel were grown

up. That made Ethel proud and happy. She knew how to sew a patch on the seat of Willie's or Charlie's overalls, too, and darn the heel of a stocking.

But tonight Ethel was looking at a dog-eared catalog. While she was over at one of the neighbors' today, she had seen the book lying on a table and picked it up. On the back it said, "Larkin Company." The neighbor lady told her she could have it if she wanted it.

"Why don't you get up an order, Ethel?" she had suggested. "You can get the nicest premiums with your orders. Their prices are a little high, I think, but you can't get better things anywhere. If you do get up an order, I'd like to have a box of that coconut oil soap."

So Ethel had brought the catalog home. Now that the dishes were washed and put away, she had a half hour before she had to go to bed. She got out an order book and wrote down the box of soap. It was a dollar to start with—if she should decide to get up an order. Just then something the pastor was saying in the other room attracted her attention.

"We'll have to use the old chairs in the church until we can buy pews," he declared. "And we'll have to wait for platform furniture, too. But having the new church will be wonderful anyway."

"Why can't we build pews ourselves?" daddy asked. "Brother Woodring is a good carpenter, and he was talking to me about pews just the other day. He said if several of us got together to sand and plane, he'd be glad to donate his time. And I think if I go out to Burns Lumber Works,

I might get some lumber donated. At least I could get it cheaper."

Now Ethel was really thinking hard. Daddy wanted to get new pews. If he decided a thing should be done, it was as good as done. He was just like old Shep with a rag. He kept worrying at it till it was finished. She wanted to be like that, too—to plan things and get them done.

She wasn't even concentrating, but she kept flipping the pages of the book. Suddenly she gasped. There in the catalog were some chairs—armchairs and straight chairs to match. She thought of the old battered chairs they had been using on the platform. It would be too bad to have such battered old things in the pretty new church. Carefully she read the description under the picture of the new chairs. "Mission wood, dull finish. Upholstered in genuine black leather. Given with a fifteen-dollar purchase of products."

Ethel got a pencil and started figuring. She would have to sell forty-five dollars' worth of things if she was going to get two straight chairs and one armchair for the new church.

Oh, it would be wonderful if she could do that! Just think—missionaries and great ministers would come to the new church and sit down on these very chairs. It would be the most wonderful thing in her life if she could help fix up the new church. But forty-five dollars was a huge sum of money. How could she ever sell that much of Larkin's things?

After she had put on her nightgown that night, she

added a shy petition to her usual prayers: "And, Lord, please help me to get a big enough order of Larkin's things to get those chairs for the church."

She almost ran her legs off getting the chores done for mother the next morning. Then she told mother her plan. She showed her the picture of the chairs, and her blue eyes gleamed with such earnestness that mother didn't have the heart to discourage her, though she wondered if Ethel could possibly get enough orders to earn the chairs.

"Why don't you fix a little lunch and go out and try right now, dear? You can have the rest of the day," she said. "The washing and the ironing are done, and you can take off and see what you can do."

Ethel buttoned on a clean, starched print dress, combed her hair carefully, and tied two pretty pink ribbons on the ends of her long braids. Taking the catalog, away she went. She was pretty well known in the neighborhood, since so many people traded at her father's store, and when she told folks that she was taking orders so that she could win the chairs for the church, they bought as fast as she could write down the orders. It was hard, though, for some folks ordered only twenty-five or fifty cents' worth. The total grew slowly.

By five o'clock that night Ethel had a blister on her heel. She had been stung by a bee and chased by a dog. She was very tired, but she had a lot of orders. She could hardly wait to get home and see how well she had done.

Mother was dishing up potato soup when Ethel plodded up the steps. A great platter of red tomato slices was at one end of the table, and a plate of fluffy biscuits, delicately brown, stood near the other end next to a bowl of homemade cottage cheese. Ethel suddenly was as hungry as a timber wolf.

The whole family was interested in what she had done, but mother said no one was going to do a thing but eat now, while things were hot. There would be time enough to see how much Ethel had gotten after the dishes were washed and put away.

Supper was a noisy meal, for everyone wanted to talk. Daddy had a lot to say about what went on in the store, and Charlie wanted to tell about a horse that ran away on Willard Street. Even little Chester wanted to talk about the old rooster that pecked him. He was even willing to get down from the table to show the red places on his leg, but mother kept him in his place.

"You just stay right there in your high chair, Chester," she said. "Ethel can see your scratches after supper."

Ethel didn't have much to say. All the time she was eating she could see the pretty chairs and the legend underneath that read, "Made of fine mission wood, dull finish. Genuine leather seats." Then daddy got to talking about the church. He told Ethel that she was just like the women who helped to embroider the veils in the tabernacle in the days of Israel, for she was working for the Lord, and He was keeping account of it in the books of heaven. Her heart swelled with joy.

After the supper things were cleared away, mother helped Ethel count up the orders. They figured out that if Ethel worked about a week, she could easily accumulate the necessary order.

"You get an early start in the morning," mother said. "I'll do up the housework, and you can get a lot done before it gets too hot."

Before the week was over, mother had helped Ethel make out the order and send it to the Larkin Company in Buffalo, New York. Then the real suspense started. Finally, a card arrived saying that the goods had arrived at the freight office. Daddy took the card and got the order that very day.

Ethel could hardly stand it until daddy came and set the big boxes on the brick sidewalk. Wonder of wonders! The company had sent the chairs, too. Ethel thought surely they would wait till she had delivered the things and sent the money back. The chairs were wrapped in burlap and excelsior. Ethel was so excited when daddy took his pocketknife, cut the strings, and pulled the chairs from the packing—right there on the sidewalk. Reverently she carried them indoors and set them in the parlor. Oh, they looked so grand and beautiful, with their genuine leather seats! She walked around them, looking at them, touching the smooth wood with gentle hands.

That evening the pastor came over to talk to daddy about the plans for dedicating the new building. It was nearly completed, and all paid for. The union conference president was coming, and there would be an all-day meeting, with folks from out in the country bringing their lunches to eat in Heekins Park. The whole church was talking about it. Daddy was so proud of Ethel's project that he had to take the pastor into the parlor to show him what she had done. Ethel was finishing up the dishes when she heard them talking. Daddy called her.

"Ethel, come in here a minute. Pastor Stone wants to see you."

Shyly Ethel went in and stood by the door.

"Ethel," the kind old man said, as he took her hand, "not many girls of your age have the ambition to help build a church. I know the Lord is pleased by what you have done. The chairs are beautiful. Many great men of God will sit in them, and your work will serve the Lord for many years. I have told your father that since you are the youngest person to help so much on the church, I would like for you to have a part in the dedication. I want you to speak a piece. My wife will be glad to help you memorize it."

"And I'll get you a brand-new dress," whispered mother, giving Ethel a quick hug and kiss.

Ethel had to run straight to her room to think about this new wonder, for girls didn't get many new dresses in those days. One good dress for winter, and one for summer, and that was all. Of course, there were nice plain ginghams and calicoes for work and school, but one good dress was all Ethel could expect. Now she would have two. It was a wonderful thing to think about.

By the end of the week Ethel had delivered all her orders and mailed the check to Buffalo. She sighed with great relief, for she had worked hard, but she was very happy. Then mother took her to the dry-goods store in town, and they bought the material for the new dress. Mother got a soft honey color that seemed to bring out the blue in Ethel's eyes. It was the color of her fluffy hair, and it looked lovely when mother held it up against her. Then, while mother was getting the uninteresting items, such as lining and belting and seam binding and hooks and eyes, Ethel wandered out and amused herself by wheeling the baby up and down in her high carriage.

On the way home, mother left the material with Mrs. Knapp, the dressmaker. She measured Ethel and looked at the goods and the pattern and promised to get the dress done in plenty of time for the dedication, which was a week and a half away.

Time flew fast now. Ethel went every day to Pastor Stone's house, and Mrs. Stone drilled her on her special piece. From there she would go to the dressmaker to have her dress fitted. On the way, she would practice her piece, so as to have it word perfect.

"Was there ever a girl so lucky?" she asked herself. Her cousins in Indianapolis were always saying how big and fine their city was, but she felt sorry for them now. They were not going to have a church dedication, nor would they get to say a piece or have a new dress.

The dress was supposed to be done on Thursday. Ethel was so excited that she almost got sick. Mrs. Knapp didn't have the dress quite done in the afternoon, so daddy said he would get it when he went that way with Mrs. Mooney's order on Thursday evening.

Supper was over, the dishes were washed, and the smaller children were in bed. And still he did not come home. Mother soothed Ethel, who was almost beside herself with worry.

"He's just met someone and gotten to talking, I'll be bound," mother said. "Men say we women are talkers—but——" and she laughed comfortably.

Ethel went out on the sidewalk to watch. Soon she heard the rumble of the wagon wheels and ran to the corner to meet her father. He had met the pastor, and the two had ridden home together. They were still deep in a discussion of the last-minute plans.

"Where's my dress, Daddy? Where's my dress?" Ethel cried before the horse even stopped.

"Over there in the back," he answered. "Mrs. Knapp pinned it up in newspapers and laid it in the back of the wagon."

Ethel reached in and felt all over the boards. The dress was not there! She climbed up on the tailgate and felt clear in under the seat. It simply was not there!

By this time, she was calling to everyone for help. Daddy lit the lantern, assuring her he was certain the dress was there. But it wasn't. It must have bounced out when the wagon hit a bump.

Ethel stood like a statue. She did not cry. She simply stood and stared. She couldn't grasp the fact that the lovely honey-colored dress she had tried on only that afternoon was gone. She would not have a new dress for the dedication.

She went into the house and up the narrow, dark stairs to her room. What was she to do? In her excitement she had bragged a little to Bonnie and Lottie and Lillian, and they were all eager to hear her speak her piece and see her new dress. She lay down on the bed, too miserable even to cry. Mother came in quietly and patted her head.

"Dear, don't feel so bad. Maybe we'll find it, though I don't want to give you much hope. It must have fallen out in the poor part of town daddy had to drive through. But we can pray, and if it is the Lord's will, we will find it. Daddy has already gone uptown to put an ad in the *Morning Star*. If an honest person finds it, we'll get it back tomorrow. Daddy feels just as bad as you do."

The next day mother helped Ethel press her regular Sabbath dress. She found some pleasure in her new shoes and stockings and her pretty new hat. But they had been bought to match the honey-gold dress, not the plain old green plaid, trimmed in tan.

Friday went by, and the dress did not come back. As Sabbath came closer and closer, a more unhappy girl would have been hard to find.

"It may be that the Lord let this happen. You *might* have been too proud of that dress," mother suggested once.

But Ethel knew her mother felt sorry for her. If it had been a day when dresses were easily bought, mother would have gone straight to town and gotten another one. But that day had not arrived, and there were very few readymade dresses in any of the stores.

Sabbath morning Ethel dressed carefully. She looked

very nice when she started out to Sabbath School—the first Sabbath School in the new church. Mother was ready to go, and the baby was taking a nap in her carriage. Then mother seemed to change her mind. "I don't think I'll go to Sabbath School," she said. "I'll stay here another hour, and then walk over with little Josephine. If she gets her nap, she's not likely to be restless during the church service. You all run ahead."

When Ethel reached Sabbath School, Lottie asked, "Where's your new dress?"

"It got lost out of the grocery wagon," Ethel whispered back, winking hard to stop her tears.

"Why, that's terrible!" Lottie answered. "I'm so sorry."

In spite of her disappointment, Ethel loved the church. The new walnut pews, the new green rug runner, the new pulpit desk. And up there, on the new green carpet, the three chairs—"solid mission wood, dull finish, genuine leather seats." She had earned them for the Lord. And her piece was to be *first* on the dedication program.

As the congregation was singing the closing song for Sabbath School, Brother Hartley touched Ethel on the shoulder.

"Ethel," he whispered, "your mother sent word for you to run home as fast as you can go."

Ethel forgot her jacket and her hat. She raced down the street, and in only a matter of minutes she was running up the front steps at home. Mother was unbuttoning her dress before she was hardly inside the door. There on the sofa lay her precious honey-gold dress.

"A lady brought it back not fifteen minutes ago," her mother was saying. "She was so poor and ragged looking that I went into the store and fixed her a market basket full of groceries—rice, sugar, bread, beans, butter. I tell you, she was pleased. She almost cried."

Intermission was over when Ethel ran up the church steps. Folks were gathering for the service. The whole lot outside was full of rigs and buggies. Mother pushed the baby buggy into a shady spot by the side of the church. Baby Josephine was still asleep. There was a brand-new reed organ, which the building committee had sent clear to Indianapolis to get. It had been paid for by donations from the young married people's class. Now Lottie was starting to play the organ. The music sounded almost as if it were from the very gates of heaven.

Ethel slipped into the front seat, where Pastor Stone had told her she should sit. Finally, Pastor Stone announced her part. He showed that big congregation the beautiful chairs—"mission wood, dull finish"—and Ethel's heart was so happy she was sure it would burst.

"And now, as our *youngest* big contributor, Ethel will have the first part on our dedication program," the pastor said.

Ethel, looking like a small angel dressed in honey-gold, climbed happily up the platform steps.

THE DIRTY BUGGY

*C*ARL WAS more excited that morning than he had ever been in his life. He took down the clean and shining milk pails, opened the kitchen door, and went out. The birds in the orchard next to the house were almost splitting their throats with the joy of daybreak. A dim light in the barn told Carl that dad was already there. Couldn't beat dad to the barn. He seemed to sleep with one eye open and his shoes on.

Carl hurried down the kitchen steps, being careful not to clank the buckets and waken grandma, whose room was near the kitchen. Today was his last day at home; his last day to milk and feed the cows, chop wood, husk corn, and do the hundreds of other things a boy gets tired of doing all the time.

According to the calendar it was the month of September, 1890. Carl was fourteen and had just graduated in May from the red schoolhouse a mile down the dirt road. Dad and mother, after a long council with grandma and Aunt Sadie and Uncle Peter, had decided he ought to go to high school. But the problem was that the nearest high school was in Mertonville, twenty miles from home.

Mertonville! Carl's heart thumped every time he thought about Mertonville. It was a huge town—twenty-five thousand people—and what seemed like hundreds of stores. So different from old Whipple's General Store in Beldon Village, where they sold codfish in salty slabs, mackerel in kegs, and kraut in barrels.

Carl went through the milking automatically, all the time thinking about the job he had gotten so that he could work after school and earn his board and keep and a little spending money. He remembered the ad: "Wanted: High school boy to care for horse and carriage for minister's family. Private room. Pleasant work. Allow time off to go to high school." He had gone with dad and Uncle Peter to see about the job. At least ten boys were already waiting to see the minister when they arrived.

The office girl told them that the minister would be right in, and asked them to wait. Then she went on with her work at the typewriter.

Carl looked at the big machine curiously. He had never seen a typewriter before. It made a lot more noise than he thought it ought to.

Several boys, tired of waiting, left after a while. Four

remained. When at last the minister, Amaziah Baxter, arrived—fat, puffing, and pompous—he gave the boys a little written examination. Carl was rather disgusted at that. It seemed a little silly to be sitting there telling on paper answers to questions such as: "Have you ever used tobacco?" "Have you carried responsibility at home?" "Name your home duties." But to his delight Carl got the job. The dignified Mr. Baxter took him and father and Uncle Peter out to show him the place where he would stay. It was a room over the carriage house, and to Carl's country eyes the furniture looked grand.

"Son," his father said, "this is a big city. There are saloons, and poolrooms, and some mighty mean people who won't stop at anything. I want you to stay away from the bad crowd. It can spoil your life."

"I will, Dad," Carl answered. "I'll promise that. You and mother have taught me to stay away from things like that, and I'm glad I never learned to like them."

"You've been brought up to go to church, too, Carl," dad added. "You must remember to keep Sunday the way we've taught you. You know we have done as little as we could on that day. Mother even does most of her cooking on Saturday. Few people keep Sunday the way they ought to."

"I promise, Dad," Carl repeated. "I never knew any other way to keep Sunday."

Carl remembered all these things as he sat down to his last breakfast at home. Mom had made buttermilk biscuits and sour cream gravy for him, because that was his favorite breakfast. But he could hardly eat, he was so excited. They would start to town right after he finished eating.

Mother, dad, and Uncle Peter helped Carl get settled in his new place. Mother put his clothes neatly in the dresser drawers. They all thought the furniture was the grandest they had ever seen. They didn't know it was furniture considered too old-fashioned and too out of date for the beautiful Baxter home. There was a great towering walnut bedstead and a wide dresser with a large mirror. A small stove had been put up to keep the room warm. A packing crate stood beside it for a woodbox.

The minister showed Carl the two fine horses that were to be his special charge, the one Jersey cow he was to milk, and the handsome carriage he was to keep spotlessly clean. It was easy—easier than the work he'd been used to at home.

"You'll have to get up at five at least, son," his father reminded him anxiously. "Do you think you can do it? I always called you at home, remember?"

Carl laughed. "Dad, I'm always awake when you call me. I'll get along all right. I can feed and water the horses and the cow, get the barn set up for the day, and that one cow milked easily by six thirty. Then I'm to go to the kitchen and eat with the cook and the yardman by seven. I can get cleaned up and to school by eight. It'll be a snap."

He looked around his quarters rather proudly. It was his first venture into the grown-up world; he was on his own now.

The next week was so full of work that Carl wondered

what he had ever done on the farm. He studied Latin, algebra, English, biology, and ancient history. His new books stood on the table by the window. He had pens, ink, pencils, paper, and some notebooks. He did his work in the stables perfectly, as he had been taught to do, and he studied every spare moment he could find.

On Saturday he spent the whole day cleaning, scouring, currying, and scraping. He did some extra studying, too. But always on Sundays he rested and just walked around town.

Of course, he went to church. At first he went to the church where his employer was the pastor for the high society of Mertonville. He felt strange about going there, for he seldom saw the dignified gentleman who had hired him except from a distance. So he tried another church, and yet another, until he found a little one with an atmosphere almost as friendly as his own church back home.

He was lonely all winter. He studied hard, made good grades, and wrote long letters home.

Several times the boys at school talked to him about poolrooms and dances, and some of them showed him cigars (few men smoked cigarettes in that day). Some of the boys hinted darkly about beer-drinking adventures. Carl, looking at the boys, felt a strong inward distaste. He had known so many boys who thought growing up was being able to do just as they pleased—doing daring, wicked things that their folks wouldn't let them do if they knew. Carl and his father had talked so often that Carl knew doing just as one pleased wasn't possible. Even dad couldn't do as he pleased. He'd often say, "When a boy grows up, Carl, a lot of serious things happen that young fellows don't think about. I can't spend just what I please because there are certain needs and bills I must meet. I can't go off the deep end and make silly purchases. I have to think things through, Carl."

So Carl had learned early to "think things through," to do the sensible thing.

The Baxters, on the other hand, had a son, Rex, whom Mrs. Baxter idolized and catered to and petted and adored.

Carl often heard her talking to the maid. "Don't clean upstairs this morning, Hilda. Rexie isn't feeling good. He mustn't be disturbed."

Carl knew what was the matter with her "Rexie." He'd been out most of the night playing cards and smoking and going to the moving picture shows. It was scandalous the way he went to school just when he got good and ready. Rex Baxter's grades were a joke even among the boys.

Rex was a dark young fellow with shifty, brooding eyes, and he never seemed happy. He had everything but cared about nothing.

"If they'd make him take care of their horse and cow, he'd be a lot happier," Carl wrote to his father and mother. "He just lounges around, restless, and he looks miserable. He'd be better off, too, if he'd study his lessons, I'm sure."

But the Baxters didn't seem to see what was plain to Carl's clear eyes and sensible thinking.

One Saturday it rained, and the streets were nothing

but mud. The carriage in which the Baxters rode was very dirty from the pastor's trips to town and to the hospitals and to the homes of church members. Carl pulled it inside the big barn and surveyed it ruefully. He'd just *have* to clean it up, but one trip would ruin it again. Outside, the downpour continued. An April rain can be cold and miserable, Carl decided.

He put on his boots, lugged a bucket of water from the pump, and got to work.

First, he took a whisk broom and cleaned out the inside thoroughly, washed the floor, rubbed and polished the metal, and brushed and shook the floor rugs. He finished up by polishing the outside, just as he did every Saturday. The pair of horses were curried, the stables were cleaned, and the Saturday night milking done before Carl felt free to clean himself up and rest and study.

Once during the night he thought he heard noises below, but he could hardly believe that someone would take the rig out in such awful weather. The minister never wanted his carriage used until Sunday morning. It continued to rain steadily and hard all night. Carl must have been sound asleep when he heard banging on his door. Was it the wind? Surely no one would want to see him at this hour! He lit a match. Why, it was only a quarter to five! But there was that knocking, right at the stair door!

Carl jumped up and went to the door and opened it cautiously. To his embarrassment, the Reverend Baxter was standing there; but he looked very different from the clean, dignified, unruffled gentleman Carl knew. He had an overcoat on over a white nightshirt. His hair was sticking up straight all over his head, and even his glasses were crooked. Carl was so shocked that he hardly knew what to say.

"My boy," began the minister, "I've some extra work for you to do this morning—right now, in fact, or you'll not be through in time for—uh—the church service."

Carl was still speechless.

The minister continued. "Unfortunately, it was necessary for Rex to use the carriage last night. He was detained because one of his friends was sick, and got caught in the storm; so you can see, my boy, the carriage needs a most thorough cleaning."

Carl finally found his voice.

"I'll go clean out the inside and fix it up as well as I can, with as little work as possible, sir," Carl said. He turned to get his work clothes that were lying on the chair.

But the minister looked puzzled. "What do you mean by 'as little work as possible,' my boy?"

Carl smiled. "I'm sure you don't want me to break the Sabbath by carrying water and scrubbing as I did yesterday, do you? I was always taught to do only the most necessary work on the Sabbath."

Mr. Baxter sat down on one of Carl's chairs and laughed.

"What do you mean, Carl, calling Sunday the Sabbath? It isn't the Sabbath!"

Carl was the puzzled one now. At the look of amazement on his face, the minister laughed again.

"Sunday's not the Sabbath?" Carl managed to gasp. "Why, of course it is!"

"No, it's not and never has been. If you're so bound to observe the Sabbath, you'll have to keep Saturday, my boy. That's the seventh day, and everyone who has a lick of sense can look at the calendar and see it."

"But how——"

The gentleman got up, a smile still on his face. "I haven't time to explain to you the details of how we came to keep Sunday, but it's just a custom that came in many years after our Lord was crucified. It is in remembrance of His resurrection. But it does no harm to do a bit of work on Sunday, Carl." And the minister went creaking down the stairs without so much as a "good-bye."

Carl was angry. A door had opened in his mind, however, through which new thoughts poured like water through a floodgate. Before he finished dressing, he went to look at the calendar. Sure enough, there it was—Saturday was the seventh day of the week. Thoughtfully he went down and scrubbed the carriage till it shone and carried out two beer bottles that had been left inside.

That afternoon Carl looked up the word *Sabbath* in the concordance of the Bible his mother had given him. Before nightfall he had decided that the minister was right.

It took time, study, and concentrated conviction, but Carl eventually found his way to the Sabbath-keeping Seventh-day Adventist Church. He had come to Mertonville for one kind of education, but he left with both it and another kind—an education for eternity.

CLARA'S SEARCH, PART I

*T*HE ROOM behind the springhouse had a little stream trickling through it over flat stones. Those stones had been placed there by slaves many years before, when dusky hands and backs bore the brunt of hard and grueling labor. But the water, still cold as ice, kept the milk in the crocks cold and the butter firm and sweet.

It was good to have this cool, dark, mossy springhouse, Clara Ann Seymor decided as she poked her nose through the door and sniffed. The Perkinses up the road didn't have one, and on hot, muggy days their pantry smelled of spoiling milk and rancid butter.

The house where Clara Ann lived was an old rambling farmhouse with climbing roses and ivy that tried their best to hide the warping boards gone bone white from lack of paint. Inside was a battleground, where Clara Ann's mother waged a continual war against dirt, flies, dust, cockroaches, and mud. Times had been so hard that it was all the Seymors could do to keep the family fed and clothed, and little was left for frills. The demands for salt, sugar, axle grease, shoes, and matches—things that could not be grown on the farm—were always more than pa's thin wallet could manage.

The red fields, carved out of a few flat pieces of barren land, produced fairly good crops; but there was little market for them. Cars had not yet begun to invade the rural areas, so there were few people in the neighborhood who didn't grow their own supplies. Roads were narrow, and almost impassable during much of the year. Butter sold for twenty cents a pound if you were lucky, but fifteen or eighteen most of the time. Eggs were dirt cheap, too, for everyone had his own hens and needed shoes worse than eggs.

Clara Ann went barefoot from April to October, except to church. She wore shoes, such as they were, on Sundays only.

Father had to hitch up the horse to the two-seated carriage to get to the church in town where he and mother were members. But often on Sundays the roads were bad, or it was too rainy or too hot or too cold, or father needed to finish up some work. They seldom went to church.

Usually mother cooked Sunday dinner a little earlier on the rare occasions when they did go. "Gives me time to get a little rest," she said. "I do declare, it's a lot easier when I don't go to church. Sunday is as hard a day as Monday."

Clara Ann was a serious girl. One of her Sunday School teachers had given her a Bible, and she read it regularly. She looked up as her mother spoke.

"It doesn't seem right, Mother," she said slowly. "I was reading the commandments this week in the Bible. And when it talks about the Sabbath, it says not to do any work that day. It says to rest. You don't get much rest on Sunday, do you, Mother?"

This kind remark from her little girl touched the busy mother's heart. "I'll say I don't," she said disgustedly. "With Sid's folks always coming out for a free chicken dinner, and with everyone just sitting around, stuffing themselves and dirtying up the house, it's the hardest day of the week for me. I'll say it isn't right."

"It shouldn't be like that, Mother," Clara Ann continued, her clear eyes puzzled. "You need to rest sometimes. I think that commandment is for you, too. I wish I could help you more."

"You help me a lot, dear." There were tears in mother's eyes. "I don't know what I would do without you. You save my legs many a step."

About a mile from the Seymors' house, back in the woods, was a small weather-beaten church. It was built of shrunken bleached-out timbers that someone said were cut from logs by hand in the days of the circuit riders.

Graves surrounded the place, untended, covered with rough, coarse grass. Some, clear in the back by the log fence, were sunk down and all but forgotten. Rosebushes with yellow flowers and sharp thorns ran wild.

Sometimes Clara Ann went back to the old part and thought about the people who were buried there. What were they like? Did they think and dream as she did? Were they in heaven watching her?

There was a girl named Vinnie Mae sleeping under a wind-strafed sunken stone. "Vinnie Mae" was crudely lettered in the thin stone, and it was so dim now that Clara Ann could hardly read it. "Aged 14. Thou wast dear and good," it said. Would Vinnie Mae be glad that they had written that about her, while she was an angel flying around in heaven now? What about the dead people? Clara Ann had read some things in the Bible that made her wonder. In one place she had read, "The dead know not any thing." Something was wrong, Clara Ann decided. But what?

She asked her mother once who Vinnie Mae was.

"Land, that Vinnie Mae!" her mother exclaimed, pushing her hair back out of her eyes and letting the sock she was darning rest for a moment in her lap. "I heard my Grandpa Cartwright talk about her. He said she was a young girl he had seen once in a while. She was killed, bit by a rattlesnake while she was picking blueberries."

It pleased Clara Ann to learn about the past and the future. She was like that, always wondering about things, never satisfied. And Clara was ambitious. She stood at the head of all her classes. It was a pity there was no high school for her to go to, for she wanted so much to learn.

"I wish even one of our *boys* was as smart as she is," pa muttered one day. "Might be, if one of them was, we could make something of him."

Clara Ann was curious about that little country church with all the graves around it. She got up early one Sunday morning and helped ma all she could. Then she put on a clean dress and walked to the meeting. She arrived after the services had started. There were a few adults, shabby and poor, and several children occupying the ancient pews. They had a few dog-eared hymnbooks and were trying to sing without any accompaniment. No one could play the old organ that sat, closed, in one corner. Clara Ann was barefoot, but so were most of the others, so she did not care. She thought to herself that even some Presidents had gone barefoot in their childhood.

Because Clara Ann honestly wanted to help, she went and opened the organ, twirled the tall stool, and sat down with a swish of her calico skirts. Her quick eyes scanned through the song until she found the measure the congregation was struggling through, and she began to play. The reedy sweetness filled the room. People began to smile and to sing with more spirit. Pleasure sparkled in the children's eyes.

Clara Ann played for all the songs that day. When the congregation broke up for class study, the superintendent came over and asked her to teach a class of five-year-old boys. He pressed a faded lesson sheet into her hand. Glancing at it, she realized that she knew the story by heart from reading the New Testament so much. It was about the healing of the crippled man by the Gate Beautiful.

She found an old blackboard. It was spotted and blotched, but with a small piece of chalk she drew a gate, and when she added a few stick men, the story began to live for the little boys. They wriggled with joy.

When the bell rang for the classes to close, one little boy pressed close to her and whispered loudly, "Come teach us again next Sunday, Clara Ann. I liked it. Sunday School hain't so long when you're here."

"I think so, too," said another. And all the other little boys agreed.

Clara Ann felt happy clear down to her toes when she walked home. At the church in town she just sat and listened. Miss Marx played the piano, and there were enough teachers without her. No one asked her to do anything. Clara Ann needed to be needed.

Every Sunday after that she trudged down the dusty road to the organ and her wistful five-year-olds. She planned for them all week. She cut out pictures and fixed up other little illustrations to help with the lesson study. She carried her things to church in a split reed basket. The children always ran to meet her.

"My turn to sit by Clara Ann!"

"No. It's mine."

" 'Taint neither. You set by her last Sunday."

One Sunday, however, Clara's family decided to go to church in town. Mother came out wearing her best voile dress and her Sunday hat.

"Come on, Clara Ann," she said.

"Please, Mother, I don't want to go to the city church. I want to go to the little church down the road. You know I've been going every Sunday."

"Yes, but that was because we couldn't get to town."

"But, Mother, I play the organ; and the little boys will miss me if I don't come."

Mother chose to make an issue of the matter.

"You must go with us, Clara Ann. I am worried about your running down to that country church. They believe in sprinkling for baptism. Our church knows better than that. Land, I don't see how people can be so ignorant of the Bible." She spat out the words as if some old bitter bug had gotten in her mouth and made her sick.

"But, Mother, they need me. I'm not needed in town. There will be no one to play the organ, and those little boys will cry if I don't come. And——"

"Clara Ann, do what your mother says," father broke in sharply.

Clara Ann burst into a torrent of tears, and her father softened a little.

"Let's let her stay, Mattie," he said. "After all, what's the difference? We've got to get going. We'll be late as it is."

Clara Ann was allowed to go that day, but her mother finally forbade her to go anymore to the little church where she was loved and needed. She cried bitterly, but her mother's lips were set in a determined line.

"We have always belonged to the town church, and we always will," she declared. "I don't like to see you mixed up with that country church, Clara Ann. It's a different denomination. First thing you know, they would be after you to be a member. Then, where would you be?"

"But they're good people, Mother."

She said it innocently enough, but her mother gasped. "Now, would you just listen to that girl! I'm sure now that it's time for you to quit trotting off down there."

Clara Ann thought a great deal about what her mother had said. Why did her folks hate and fear the other churches? She had visited some of them when she got a chance, which wasn't often. One thing struck her. Every church seemed to think that its way was the right way to heaven. Yet they all taught something different. There must be just *one* right way, she reasoned.

With no high school near enough to attend, nowhere she could go to work, and with no one on earth to encourage her to do anything different, Clara Ann did what all the neighborhood girls did—she drifted into an early marriage.

There was a young man who occasionally attended Clara's church in town. He was handsome and full of fun. He had a job in a print shop, always had money to spend, and he wore better clothes than most of the other boys. To Clara's inexperienced eyes he was a fascinating creature. He began to court her, and that pleased her very much. Clara didn't realize it, and would have denied it if someone had told her, but she was a very pretty girl.

Clara thought that living in town would be pretty much like living in heaven. She wouldn't have to milk the cows twice a day; she could go to the store whenever she needed something instead of once or twice a month; she could have close neighbors, go to church every Sunday, and have a chance to attend everything that went on in town. All of this seemed like an enchanted fairyland. When Carl asked her to marry him, she accepted quickly.

There was a moving picture theater in town. Clara Ann saw the movies for the first time with Carl before they were married. Her conscience bothered her at first, for there were some in the church who said that the theater was a wicked place. But Carl laughed at her and pinched her cheek.

"Little Puritan," he teased pleasantly. "I'll get you over feeling conscience-smitten by such little things. The trouble with you is that you never had a good time in all your life. I'll show you what fun life can be when we get married. Churches are not the stodgy old places they used to be. They let a person have a good time. They know they have to, or they wouldn't have any members. Folks don't like to be considered odd."

"But, Carl," Clara Ann said, "I think Christians should be different from the world. I think we should be separate, or something. I think I read in the Bible that——"

"Clara, you really *are* old-fashioned. I wouldn't be a bit surprised to hear you say that even smoking is wrong. Well, I smoke, and I like it. It's fun and relaxing. I happen to know that the Reverend Carr from our own church enjoys his after-dinner cigar. Now, what does that have to do with religion, Little Miss Prude?"

Clara Ann had no answer ready. She knew of several of the church members who smoked, or chewed, or dipped snuff, and no one said a word about it. Yet, somehow, she just knew it wasn't right.

She talked to her mother once about smoking.

Looking at her sharply, her mother said, "If you're wondering about smoking because Carl smokes, let me just say this: If smoking is all your husband ever does for you to complain about, you're lucky. Smokin' ain't nothing. But let your man get to drinking or gambling, then I'd say you'd have something to complain about."

Her mother kept on washing the dishes, thoughtfully. Then she continued talking:

"Well, by some people's way of thinking, smoking is wrong. I remember when I was a girl, a preacher in our church said it was an evil thing. Even so, there were other preachers who spat out a quid at the door before they went in to preach. I don't know as there's a church anywhere that does exactly what the Lord wants them to do."

"Now there you are," Clara Ann thought. "Surely there must be one church somewhere that does the whole will of the Lord."

Clara Ann was soon busy getting ready to have her own home. She didn't realize that the Holy Spirit was bringing these troublesome thoughts to her mind.

Later on, after her marriage, the neighborhood girls envied her. Her little house in town was furnished with brand-new furniture, and she had new dishes and rugs and pots and kettles and linens.

As the months went by, she realized that under her surface happiness there was a constant feeling of sadness. Ever since she was a small girl she had always felt it was important to do what she thought was right. Now she had slipped into the groove of living Carl's kind of life.

Before long two little girls and a boy enlarged their family circle. Clara was glad, because now she had to stay home and take care of them, and she had a real excuse not to go to the show as regularly as Carl wanted her to.

Once, when the first baby was tiny, Carl said one night, "Come on, Clara, let's go to a show."

"What about the baby?" Clara asked. "She might cry."

"No, she won't. You know she hardly ever cries. I'll carry her."

That night was the first in a series of strange events that changed Clara's whole life. As she sat in the theater, holding her baby and watching the imaginative love affair flickering on the screen, it seemed as if a voice spoke to her: "You're a pretty example for a little baby girl, Clara Ann. Aren't you ashamed?"

Clara Ann gasped. Her baby's little face looked so innocent in the flickering light. Suddenly Clara was terrified. What if the place caught fire, and she and the baby were burned up? What if they were trampled to death trying to get out like people were in that terrible Iroquois Theater fire in Chicago?

Right there, clutching little Beth in her arms, Clara made a solemn vow, one she never broke, though she suffered for it. If God would forgive her and let her get safely home with little Beth, she would never go to a theater again. A strange peace came over her. She sat thinking quietly during all the rest of the film and never knew how the story ended.

On the way home she told Carl what had happened to her. She was so happy about it that she wanted to share her joy with him.

To her surprise, Carl went into a rage. His shouts echoed down the quiet street. "Clara Ann, I'm surprised at you. You're worse than someone's old grandmother. A person would die of dry rot if he didn't have a little recreation. And a man likes to have his wife go places with him. I'm not going to be treated like a stepchild, Clara. Don't you forget that."

Her heart froze inside. She shook with fear as she turned and looked at her husband. He looked very angry, and there was a white ridge along his jaw that she had noticed several times before when he got very angry. But he was not through lashing out at her.

"Besides, Clara, don't we go to church every Sunday? I know a lot of guys who never even stick their heads inside a church door. You're pretty mean if you refuse to go to a show with me when I go with you to church every Sunday like an obedient puppy."

CLARA'S SEARCH, PART II

*T*HEY WALKED along silently for a while. Clara was so unhappy that she thought her heart would burst. Carl was carrying baby Beth. It was a chilly early fall night. Dry leaves swirled down the street, blown by a fresh wind. They crunched when Clara stepped on them. Most of the houses were dark, but lights burned in one or two bedrooms.

"Besides, Clara"—Carl was taking up the issue again like a dog shaking a rag—"I can't see so much of your old Christianity in the churches. Look at Deacon Finnegan. Everyone knows he sells bootleg whiskey, but he goes to church every Sunday, and people think he's a pillar of the church. Ha! Look at Brother Mills, too. He owns that string of houses over by the mill; and I tell you, Clara, he practically persecutes those poor people who live there. I'd be ashamed to do some of the things he does. But he's a big man in the church!"

Clara didn't answer Carl, but every word he said added to the growing conviction in her young heart that there must be a church somewhere that was different.

As she did her housework during the weeks that followed, she pondered the problem. There must be a church somewhere that frowned on tobacco, liquor, shows, and card playing. She didn't feel that the way members of her church lived was the way to heaven. If it was, then the Bible was wrong—and Clara Ann did not believe that her Bible could be wrong.

Churchgoing was no longer a pleasure. Clara began to look at people through Carl's eyes. He had opened a whole new avenue of thought to her.

"This absolutely cannot be the right church," she told herself. "If it were, you would see a difference between the members and the rest of the world. But I can't see that Mrs. Peterson, who doesn't go to church at all, is any worse than Mrs. Carnes, who goes every Sunday."

Carl seemed to accept the idea that with the three children to look after, Clara could not go to shows with him anymore, but he continued to go anyway.

As Clara looked at her little girls and her small boy, so sturdy and sweet, her heart overflowed with love for them. She reasoned that for their sakes she must try to live the perfect life if she could. And she kept trying constantly. One day, while she was scrubbing the kitchen floor, she wrung out the rag and clasped her hands together anxiously. "What is the true way, dear Lord?" she prayed earnestly. "Please help me find it."

She continued to go to church, and Carl went with her when he felt like it. But quite often he told her he was just too dog-tired to go and hear a few old people get up and tell how good they were. That made Clara unhappy, but she would get the children ready and take them anyway. Children should not be raised without God, she told herself.

One night Carl came home excited. There was going to be a big Halloween celebration in the church basement. Clara had not attended church the Sunday before because little Beth was sick. The program, Carl said, was to raise money for a new church building. The whole church was groaning under the burden of the fund-raising campaign. But Carl told Clara that the Halloween party was going to be great, and he for one did not intend to miss it.

"Miss Fitch and Mrs. Schooter both told me to tell you to fix all the food you can to sell." He laughed. "I call that pretty good! Us fixin' a whole load of stuff to sell, and then buying it all back. Oh, well, anything to make a little money.

Instantly Clara remembered a text she had read from one of the Gospels: "My house shall be called the house of prayer; but ye have made it a den of thieves."

The text weighed her heart down like a piece of lead all that week. On Saturday she made a big cake, a dish of potato salad, and a large bowl of hickory-nut cookies.

Granny Prout came to stay with the children, and she and Carl started out together to walk to the church. Carl carried the huge basket filled with their contributions to the bazaar.

It was frosty out, and Clara welcomed the warm air in the entry of the church. But she noticed that several of the men standing just inside the door were smoking, and the air was heavy with the smell of tobacco.

They entered the basement recreation room. It was decorated with Halloween colors, orange and black, and was crowded with people. In the center of the room tables almost groaned under the heavy load of goodies. A bingo game was going on spiritedly in one corner. The prizes were hams, donated by a local packing house.

In another corner several men and women were gathered around a wheel, taking chances on white elephants that people had brought to be sold. Two or three of the girls had rigged up a kissing booth, decorated with pierced hearts and cupid's bows and arrows.

Clara stood in the door surveying the whole scene. And again that voice she had heard in the theater seemed to speak right to her. "This is not right."

"No," Clara answered, as if someone had really spoken. "No, I don't think it is."

"Come on, Clara!" Half a dozen hands were pulling at her and her basket. "Paul Simpson said he'd give two dollars for one of your cakes. Unpack your basket! Hurry, let's get going. We're really making the money tonight."

Unwillingly, Clara was pulled into the tide of the

party. She was carrying a quivering bowl of Jell-O from one table to another when she passed a knot of men to which Carl had attached himself. She heard someone say, "Listen, I really heard a good one the other day——" And from the laughter and the nudging and the lowered voices, Clara knew it was probably not the kind of joke one ought to tell. Clara shuddered.

After an hour Clara saw that all of her things had been sold. "They just went like hot cakes," one lady told her. "Guess folks know who are the good cooks around here. You ought to have made twice as much. It's for the Lord, you know."

Gathering up her dishes and packing them neatly in the basket, Clara wasn't so sure it *was* for the Lord. How could all this please a Saviour who said, "Blessed are the pure in heart: for they shall see God"?

"This is not the way." She heard the inner voice again. She looked around at all the people. They were laughing, talking, dishing out food on plates, and exchanging recipes.

"They don't know how terrible I feel," Clara thought. "What if I would scream out, 'Listen, everyone, this place should be a house of prayer. We are making it a den of thieves'? What would they say if I did that? They'd all be angry. They'd tell me I was crazy. Maybe I am. I know I will be if I stay here any longer."

She made her way quietly to Carl and touched him on the arm. "I'm going home, Carl," she whispered. Her face was so white and frightened that he turned and looked at her in alarm.

"What's the matter, honey? Feelin' sick?"

"No, Carl, at least I don't think I'm sick. But I don't like it here. This is not the way people ought to act in a church. It does make me sick in a way. It's more like a carnival midway than a church."

Angrily Carl reached out and shook her. "Clara, you're just jealous because I went over and kissed a couple of those girls. You know it didn't mean a thing! I just did it because all the rest were doing it to help the building fund. I—"

"No, Carl, that's not why. I didn't even know you had kissed them. I just feel like we are doing wrong being here. I—"

By now, he was getting uncontrollably angry, and she could see again the little white ridge along the edge of his jaw. He seized her arm and pinched it so tight that she winced with the pain.

"Clara"—he spoke in a measured voice so full of anger it trembled—"Clara, if you don't quit making a spectacle of yourself and trying to make out like you're better than everyone else, you are going to end up in the nut house. You're no angel yourself. Now settle down and have a good time like the rest of the women."

She felt tears stinging her eyes as she turned away. Quietly she finished packing her basket and went home, crying all the way. But out in the air, with the stars shining down on her, she felt cleaner and better than she had in the smoke-filled basement.

Carl was angry with her for several days and delighted

in making hateful, cutting remarks. Finally he quit, and things settled down—outwardly. But Clara's heart was more troubled than ever.

Clara finally decided that she must not be truly converted. She couldn't understand the people who said, "I've been saved for thirty years," and "Once in grace, always in grace." She had heard Old Man Stovall say that again and again, and she knew for a fact that he got drunk every time he got his paycheck. She had heard Pastor Martin tell a man that if he did not join the church and get saved he would burn in hell throughout all the ages of eternity. That was hard to figure out, too.

The next Sunday afternoon was so bright and sunny that Clara bundled up the children and let them go outside to play. The house was clean and quiet, for Carl always went to town and hung around the drugstore with his friends on Sunday afternoons. She could hear her children laughing and saw them rolling playfully in a pile of dry leaves as she went to get her Bible. She laid it on a chair and knelt beside it. She had opened it to the third chapter of John. "Ye must be born again," she read.

She was so filled with despair that tears poured down her face. She trembled. She felt that if she did not get relief from the dreadful burden of her sins, she would die.

"Lord, give it to me right now." She clasped her hands together so tight that her knuckles turned white.

Clara was to remember that hour always. Instantly the burden disappeared, and a welcome sweetness filled her soul. The whole room seemed full of holiness and blessing.

"You have answered me, Lord. Oh, You have answered me!" Tears of joy ran down her cheeks. Even the room looked different. She went outside and called the children. "Mamma loves you. Mamma loves you," she cried, and the little ones showered her with kisses and tried to tell her about the fun they were having.

So Clara entered into another phase of her journey toward grace. All of the hard things in the past seemed insignificant compared with the joy she was having in Jesus.

One day a woman came to the house to ask her assistance with the young people of the church. "You seem to be able to interest young people," the lady said. "I just thought that if we had some lively parties in the church basement—a dance or two once in a while—and if we older ones could be there and take sandwiches, we might save our young people from going to other places of amusement."

"Do you think it's right to have dances in the church?" Clara asked.

The woman dropped her head. "Well, I don't exactly like it, but if we can keep our young people interested in the church that way, I figure the end justifies the means. They are bound to dance anyway, and if they dance at the church, it's better, don't you think? Could you make a basket of sandwiches? The rest of us are fixing things. The church will furnish the coffee. We'll let the kids buy their own Cokes. And if they buy the sandwiches, it will be that much more toward the new building."

Clara was making a sweet potato cobbler at the time, so she didn't say too much. After her visitor left, she put the pastry in the oven and knelt down right there in the kitchen with the dough still on her hands. Suddenly, she knew she would never be saved in the church she belonged to. She knew that young people could never be lured to heaven by a basket of sandwiches, or by a dance or a bingo game, even though they were held in the church. Just being in a church did not make a bad thing good. Again she prayed for a specific thing.

"Lord, show me the right church. Show it to me, and I will follow it if it takes my whole life." She prayed again and again while the tears dropped from her sad face onto the clean, shiny linoleum.

Again, a feeling of peace filled her soul, and she knew that the answer was on its way.

A few days went by. Clara was in the backyard raking leaves. Since that prayer on the kitchen floor, she had prayed many times a day that the Lord would show her how to live. Carl was angry with her all the time now, and she did not know which way to turn. "If ever I needed help, I need it now, Lord. You have taken me this far. Please send someone to help me understand."

She heard someone knocking on the front door. As she went around the house, she saw an old woman who had just about the kindest face that Clara had ever seen.

Later she learned that Mrs. Philmon was out to get her Ingathering goal. But Clara had never heard of such a thing then. The lady's voice was warm and sweet as she talked to Clara about the paper she took from her purse.

"Good afternoon," she said, a smile crinkling her kind old features. "I'm Mrs. Philmon, and I live over on the next street. You see, if we read the Bible, we know that Jesus is coming soon, and we want to get ready——"

Clara was so excited that she could hardly talk, for on the paper the lady was holding out to her was a picture of Christ's second coming. Suddenly the words tumbled out. "I wonder if you would come and teach me my Bible." She sounded out of breath, she was so excited. "I've been going to church all my life, but the way I know is not the true way. I want to know what the Bible means and what it teaches."

I first met Clara at a Pathfinder camp-out. There she told me this story of her search for the right way.

She was a nurse by this time, and she seemed to be always on duty. Her bright brown eyes were ready to seek out those who were sick at heart as well as those whose bodies were ill.

Her eyes filled with tears as she finished her story.

"I lost everything. Carl did not like my struggles to do right before. Now, when I started to keep the Sabbath, his rage was uncontrollable. I wondered sometimes if he would strike me, he was so furious. I know now that he was trying every way he knew to force me back to the old easy way we had followed before. But I could not have gone back any more than a newly hatched chick could crawl back into an egg.

"He came home one day filled with a quiet, trembling rage. 'Are you really going to go to church on Saturday?' he asked. 'Are you going to continue making a fool out of me in front of the whole town?'

" 'Carl,' I said, 'I don't mean to do that. I——'

"But he interrupted. 'Answer me, Yes or No. I want to know, right now!'

"Suddenly great strength possessed me, and peace settled over me. I looked him straight in the eye.

" 'Yes, Carl,' I said. 'God helping me, I'm going to keep the Sabbath.'

" 'Then I will leave it to God to help you,' he sneered, still trembling with rage. 'Pack your things and the children's, and get out.'

"When I went to the bedroom to pack our clothes, I felt such joy that even I did not understand it. I seemed to be blind, standing on the road before Damascus, asking, 'Lord, what wilt thou have me to do?'

"Carl gave me ten dollars and a ticket to Atlanta.

" 'That's that,' he said, shrugging his shoulders. 'When you come to your senses, you can come home. Don't come before.' "

And Clara went out, like Abraham, not knowing whither she went.

The years have come and gone, filled with sweetness. Clara reared and educated her children in the church. And because it cost her so much to go all the way with God, she is constantly on the lookout for groping souls seeking their way to Him.

LEFT BEHIND

*B*ECKY PERCHED thoughtfully on the side of her bed. She almost always went to her room when she needed to think things over. She could think better there than downstairs where John was racing around with an old rag making Shep bark and Chester was whistling some old tune over and over.

Becky loved her pretty pink room. The iron bed was enameled a shining white, set off with a smooth pink bedspread and a fluffy tufted quilt. The wallpaper was covered with pink climbing roses, and sometimes Becky imagined she was in a rose arbor till she looked out the window and saw the busy street below.

Becky's day had been unhappy in a way, yet it was hard to tell just how. Part of the problem was her secret

shame at being different from the crowd. She hated to say
a word about it, for daddy was so proud to get his Bible
and walk to church every Sabbath, as if he wanted the
whole town to see that he was going to church on the day
they thought was the busiest in the week. Then, when the
girls up the street came into her father's store, she could
never join in their chatter. They would talk about the
latest show at the Bijou, their favorite movie star, the do-
ings at the rink, hot dogs, hamburgers, and Cokes. It was
a world into which Becky had never stepped, and right
now she was ashamed that it seemed so attractive.

There was a place down the road called the Cokey
Corner, where girls and boys got together and danced to
the juke box, ate hamburgers, and drank Cokes and coffee.
Becky heard them talking about it offhandedly, like—"Ha,
you should have seen how Bill acted at the Cokey Corner.
He just sat, mad at everyone, and wouldn't even dance
with Sherry; and he *is* mad when he won't dance. The rest
of us listened to the game—but Bill, ha!"

Every minute Becky felt more left out and awkward
and different. And she didn't want to be. She felt a burning jealousy, a panicky feeling that life was getting away
and she was not having all the fun she should. Of course
next year she would graduate from church school and go
to the academy. That would be fun, but that was too far in
the future. Bea and Sue and Janet always laughed at her
for going to the church school, since it had only one room
and one teacher, and especially since the big Garfield
School was two blocks nearer her home.

"Imagine!" Sue said once. "Becky goes to a school where there are only seventeen kids. Can you feature that? I'd go wild, I'd be so bored." And Becky had felt sorry for herself when Sue said that, even though Chester retorted indignantly, "Huh. You don't have near as much fun as we have. Even the teacher comes out and plays ball with us. We roast potatoes on the stove, and heat soup on cold days, and build snow forts. We have lots of fun."

Sue looked questioningly at Becky. "Do you really do that, Becky?"

"Oh, sure, and a lot more. We do have fun, really."

Becky felt a little twinge of shame that she had not taken up for the church school the way Chet had. He wasn't afraid of "those old girls," he had told her indignantly.

But today something had happened that made Becky's face burn when she remembered it. Dad had asked her to go to the wholesale house to pay a bill for him and leave an order. She had walked, for it was a pretty day, and she was allowed to keep the bus money whenever she walked.

On the way back, on an impulse, she stopped in at Bea's house. It was a small cottage, crammed close to a dozen others all built just alike. It was not a very well-kept place, and Becky knew her parents would not be too pleased about her going there, but that just made her feel all the more daring.

Bea was in the sitting room reading a magazine when Becky arrived. A brand-new stereo occupied a prominent place in the dingy room. Becky secretly imagined what mother would say if the living room at home looked like this one. She would probably say, "Becky, get the vacuum and dustcloth and scrub brush, and let's get to work."

The stereo was blaring out a rollicking, coaxing, teasing tune. It set your toe tapping, though Becky knew it was not good music. Dad and mother both liked what they called the old masters—Beethoven, Tchaikovsky, and Handel. But now Becky was excited, as if she were "one of the gang" at last, listening eagerly to the jumbled, jerky rhythm. Suddenly Bea grabbed Becky's arm.

"Come on and dance," she said. "That music really gets to me. We play it all the time at Cokey Corner, and I learned a new step the other night. I want to get some practice."

Before Becky could protest that she didn't know how to dance, she found herself being guided to the rhythm in perfect time. Her clumsy feet began to feel graceful and dainty, and to her own amazement she was dancing as easily as Bea.

Flushed and excited, Bea put on another record. "Let's do a waltz now," she said. "You surely learn fast. I'd swear you had danced before. Now look sharp. This is the way this one goes." And the gay strains of the waltz filled the room while Bea instructed Becky as if she were the final authority on everything that went on in a ballroom.

Becky's cheeks were red with excitement, and her eyes sparkled as she glimpsed herself in the mirror by the door. In all her fourteen years she had never done anything so exciting.

"There," Bea said, laughing breathlessly, "let's rest. My, your folks would drop dead if they could see you now. Hm-m-m. You surely take to dancing like a fish takes to water. Your folks shouldn't try so hard to keep you from having a good time."

Becky knew she should answer right back and tell Bea she *did* have a good time. She should have told her about the fun they had at the church socials and on Sabbath afternoons when they went for hikes in the country, or on Sundays when they went to grandpa's and played in the pond. But she didn't say a word, and Bea went on, encouraged by her silence.

"I'll give you more dancing lessons. First thing you know, you can sneak out to Cokey Corner, and if you play it right, pretty soon you'll be good enough to go to Patterson Hall. That's my big ambition. We'll go together. You'd love it, the way you got started today."

Before long Becky went home. In her room she reflected. That mention of Patterson Hall disturbed her, for everyone in town knew what had happened there. Only two houses away from daddy's store lived the Haywarden family. Erma Haywarden had been murdered in Patterson Hall by her drunk boyfriend, who thought she had danced too long with another man. The town had been shocked by Erma's death, and there had been talk for a while of closing Patterson Hall, but nothing had come of it.

So, Becky thought, Bea wanted her to go to Patterson Hall. It was Bea's *ambition* to dance well enough to go there. Ambition? How could she have an ambition like that? Becky's ambition was to be a teacher or an artist. She had tried to copy all the pictures in *The Youth's Instructor,* and even in the *Little Friend.* But Bea's ambition was to dance at Patterson Hall!

Becky still felt flattered that she had learned to dance so fast. Why did dancing have to be wrong? Didn't David dance before the Lord? She had read it in the Bible just the other day. And why on earth was it so wrong to wear jewelry? The purple earrings Bea was wearing matched her purple dress exactly. She always wore some kind of beautiful shoes, high heeled and sparkly. Becky looked at her own brown loafers. She had liked them so well the week before. Now they looked as stylish as a pair of combat boots beside Bea's elegant footwear.

Bea had glimpsed the tinsel and the glitter of one kind of world, and it dazzled her. She told Becky that at Patterson's you danced with *men,* not just silly boys like those at Cokey Corner—"if you know what I mean," she had added significantly.

Deep inside her, Becky *knew* she would never, never go to Patterson's. Dancing in the living room was one thing, but Patterson's was going way too far.

Becky heard mother call her, and she knew it was time to go down and help get supper. Even walking into the neat dining room reminded her of the contrast with the dining room she had been in that afternoon. A big bowl of begonias sat on the table in a riot of pink bloom. The everyday dishes were behind shining glass in the cupboard. Mother would never let Becky do anything carelessly, even for everyday. The table must be set just right. Silver must not be put on carelessly, and the cloth must never be messy.

Becky set the silver precisely, just as she had seen it fixed in a magazine.

But all the time she was doing her chores, Becky was keeping a secret, and it wasn't a nice secret, either. What if she suddenly spoke up during supper and said, "I can dance. Bea Morgan taught me how this afternoon while I was on my way home from town. I used to think I was awkward, but now I know I can dance just as well as the rest of the kids." She could imagine how dad would raise his brows and turn his honest blue eyes on her guilty face.

Mother would say, "Oh, Becky! Why, you know what kind of people Bea and her folks are! Shouldn't you try to show them a better life instead of——" And there would be tears in her eyes, Becky knew.

Chester and John would be just plain disgusted. No, it was not something any of them would understand, even if she told them she never intended to go to Patterson Hall or to Cokey Corner.

Dad would say, "You don't know what you would do, Becky, once you let the camel get his head in the tent."

During supper, Dad started to tell about some of the experiences Elder Stahl was having at the Lake Titicaca Mission. Dad had read about them that day in the new *Review*. All of a sudden Becky could hardly stand to think about what she had done that afternoon.

"Are you sick, Becky?" mother asked. "You're not eating. You're just pecking at your food, and you're so quiet and withdrawn."

"I don't feel very well," Becky admitted. "My head aches a little."

"Yes." Chet gave her a sidewise glance. "She certainly isn't like herself tonight. Quiet. That's not like her." And he laughed loudly, much to Becky's concern.

"Maybe it was that long walk out from town," mother speculated. "You ought to help her with the dishes, Chet. She doesn't look well."

Chet changed his mind then and tried lamely to say that he was sure Becky *was* all right, and he really had something he *had* to do, but he ended up drying the dishes just the same.

"Someday they'll make a machine that'll blow wind on dishes to dry them," Chet prophesied glumly, rubbing too hard on one plate and too little on the next one.

"Yes, and leave them all smeary," Becky answered. "Polish them, Chet. You're not shining them. They'll be streaked."

At mother's suggestion, Becky went to bed early. While she was undressing in the soft light that filtered in from the street lamp, she thought of Elder Stahl, far away in South America, making the world a better place by his good life. Before she knelt down to pray, she decided that she would try never, never to yield to temptation again. It was as if Elder Stahl had lit a lamp for her to see by.

Lying between cool, smooth sheets, she thought of Bea's untidy home. Becky had allowed Bea to think that she was unhappy with the life she lived with her parents, and wanted to escape. But she didn't, really. She loved church school, and Sabbath School, and the way Elder Dunn made things so plain in his sermons. She loved the socials, when Mrs. Carlysle made such good gingerbread all crunchy with pecans and rich with raisins and dates. Mrs. Sparry always brought a salad you cut in squares that looked like cake. There were Sabbath School picnics in the park, too; and sometimes the whole church went to Buck Creek with big fat market baskets full of food. While the children waded and paddled in the water, the men played horseshoes, and the big girls and boys played croquet or ball.

Then there was one special dream Becky liked to think about often, just before she went to sleep. The thought had begun with Elder Stahl's stories and had grown as she read Elder Thurber's wonderful book called *Min Din*. She dreamed of going to some far-off mission field and really working to help people. She dreamed about the folding organ she would take with her so that she could play good gospel hymns. "I really must get in more practice," she murmured as she dropped off to sleep.

As she slept, it seemed as if her pretty pink room was suddenly a blaze of dancing, glowing light. Becky jumped from her bed. The light was so bright that it lit up the pictures on the wall and sparkled in the mirror on the dresser. What was it? Was there a house on fire somewhere? The light seemed to get brighter all the time.

"Mother!" Becky called in alarm. No answer. She ran

into her parents' room. The bedding was thrown back, as if both her parents had left the room in a hurry. She looked into her brothers' room. They, too, were gone. But Chet's shirt and his blue pants were on one of the chairs and John's clothes lay nearby.

Becky ran downstairs, so scared that she was shaking. She grabbed the knob on the side door. It was usually hard to open, but it opened easily now. She ran across the porch onto the lawn, where the light seemed almost blinding. All the neighbors were out in the sideyard. There was Mrs. Thornburg and old grandma, Dessie George, Mr. and Mrs. Starner, and all of the Bales family. No one paid any attention to Becky. They stood absolutely still, and all of them were looking up. Becky saw her father, his face covered with smiles. Mother was beside him, holding fast to John's hand. She was smiling, too.

Dragging her eyes from their faces, Becky looked up. Her heart plunged with an awful fear. The thing was happening that she had heard about all her life. The Lord was coming! She heard music, far away, but clear and sweet. The clouds looked as if they were in a double row of steps, and down each side came glorious beings with silver trumpets in their hands. In the center, oh, it was Jesus, the King, in a blaze of glory so bright Becky had to look away; yet she longed to look again, He was so beautiful.

Then something happened that made the girl throw herself to the ground screaming. She saw her father, her mother, John, and Chester, and many of the other people suddenly begin to rise up in the air to meet the Lord.

Dad had his arms outstretched, and he was already higher than the limbs of the elm tree. She jumped up and stretched with all her might to go up, too.

"Don't leave me here!" she shrieked. "Don't leave me! Don't!" And in that dreadful moment, her distraught eyes searched the crowd, and she saw poor Bea there, stretched toward heaven, too, and crying.

"Don't leave me here," she screamed again. "Don't! Don't! Don't!"

"Wake up, dear." It was mother's voice. "Becky, dear, you're crying. Wake up, dear. Do you feel sick?"

It was morning, and the bright sunlight lay like yellow chiffon on the foot of her bed. Becky sat up. Suddenly she was happy because she knew there was still a chance to make sure she would never be left behind. There was still a chance to be proud of her faith and to let everyone know she was proud of it.

"No, Mother," Becky answered. "I'm not sick. I had a terrible dream. Mother, I dreamed that Jesus came and I was left behind."

Mother put her arm around Becky. "You won't be, Becky. The Lord has something important for you to do. You must get ready for His work, dear."

Becky picked up her bathrobe. "Mother," she said, "I wish you'd invite Bea over here. She has a terrible home-life. I feel sorry for her. She doesn't know how much fun *we* have. All she knows about is dancing and shows and records on her stereo. Our life has so much more to it than that. I think she'd like it if we showed her the way."

IRVING AND THE BESETTING SIN

*I*RVING had gone to the swimming hole after his grandmother had told him he couldn't go, and now grandfather was lecturing him.

"It's your besetting sin, that's what it is, son," grandfather was telling him seriously.

Irving squirmed. He didn't like grandfather's lectures. He just kept on and on, with absolutely no letup. You just had to listen.

Sometimes grandpa got excited enough over something Irving had done to get the shiny old razor strop down from its nail beside the comb-case mirror. Irving writhed at the thought. Grandpa wasn't weak, and that strop stung like bees through his thin overall pants.

"I tell you, Irving, I've got to break you of this disobedience if I have to——" Then both of them looked significantly at the big strap hanging there as if it were waiting to teach Irving a lesson or two.

Irving came to his grandfather's farm from the city every summer. His mother liked to have him go, and he was always eager to get back to the fields and meadows. Of course, grandpa was a great person, but it didn't do to disobey him or grandma very much.

Today was so hot. The thermometer had been pushing ninety all day. Right after he'd eaten a big dinner—grandma's apple pie, baked potatoes, corn on the cob, homemade bread, and a big salad of tender little lettuce leaves straight from grandma's garden—Corky Peters had come over.

"Come go swimmin', Irv," he had shouted just as they finished eating.

"Not so soon after dinner, Irving," grandma had said. "It isn't safe. Mick Butterfield sank like lead with a cramp and drowned last summer before anyone could get to him. He went in right after lunch, too."

Irving didn't say a word, but he thought in his heart about how foolish old people got sometimes. Drown? How dumb! He could swim like a fish.

So he had gone outside with Corky. It was so hot that the heat shimmered above the road like steam mixed with thick dust. Even the old black hens walked around with their wings raised up a little and their mouths open.

Shep lay under the willow by the well platform and panted. Down the hill toward the fringe of trees that bordered the creek, Irving could see the flashing blue of the cool flowing stream. How good the water would feel caressing his itchy, hot body!

All morning he had helped grandpa hoe in the cornfield. The big flies bit constantly at his arms and neck, and grandpa predicted cheerfully that it was a sure sign of rain. Sweat ran in jagged rivulets down his back and face and dusty arms and legs.

"C'mon," Corky whispered. "They won't know. Your grandma's gone to the summer kitchen, and I saw your grandpa go into the horse barn a minute ago. Swim a few minutes and come back, and they won't be any the wiser."

So Irving had gone, just for a minute, and now grandpa had to rave all day. How was Irving to know that grandpa was going just at that moment to the blackberry patch that bordered the creek so that grandma could make blackberry shortcake for supper? He'd no sooner jumped in the creek than grandpa, looking as avenging as old Father Time with his long beard, appeared on the bank.

Irving crept out then, naked and ashamed, and struggled back into his dusty trousers. Grandpa had lectured him all the way to the farmhouse. Then in grandma's clean kitchen, in full view of the dangling leather strop——

A fly buzzed insistently against one of the windowpanes. Muffy, the yellow and white tabby cat, lay on the braided rug in front of grandma's big wood stove.

"Irving," grandpa was saying, his kind blue eyes clouded with concern, "I'm going to lay on the strop this time, but before I do, I'm going to tell you why."

Irving's heart sank. He wasn't going to escape after

all, and that razor strop hurt just like stinging hornets. Grandpa had a strong arm for his seventy-five years.

"I wasn't a day older'n you are, Irving; and I was born on this very farm. I showed you one day right where the cabin stood where my mother kept house seventy-five years ago."

Irving's interest perked up, in spite of his dread of grandpa's punishments.

"Was it where that big yellow rosebush and the lilac bushes are, over in the field?" he asked.

"Yes," grandpa answered, his eyes mellowed by memory. "Ma said she brought those little bushes in homemade pots when they drove a wagon here from New York."

Then the old man turned his eyes back to the boy again.

"It was hot, just like today, the summer I was ten, Irving. That was sixty-five years ago. My ma didn't have a nice kitchen like this." Grandpa's eyes rested on the big polished stove, the iron sink with the cistern pitcher pump, the big glass-doored cupboard, the screen doors, the lamps—clean and filled—in a row on the shelf behind the door.

"Ma made her own candles by pouring wax into molds. I've seen her many a time. She cooked over a fireplace. Pa made her a good crane to swing the pot right over the log. She thought it was real handy.

"We'd had corn pone, and string beans, and roastin' ears, baked before the open fire that day. Me and Lemmie, my little brother, had found wild strawberries over on that hill yonder, and we had them for dinner, too. I remember everything we did that day, for it was the last day of Lemmie's life."

"Lemmie? I never heard of Lemmie," Irving stammered, embarrassed by the tears slipping down grandpa's wrinkled old cheeks.

"No, you never saw him. We never had a picture of him, only the one I carry in my memory. He had yellow hair and blue eyes. His hair was sunburned, and he had a big stone bruise on one of his toes. I remember noticing the bandage when pa pulled him out of the creek."

"Oh, was he drowned, Grandpa?" Irving gasped as he asked it.

"He was, Irving; and it was my fault. Pa told me not to go into the water so soon after a big meal. But, oh, I was smart! I knew a lot more than pa and ma—so I took Lemmie, and we sneaked down there.

" 'Course, we didn't think anything could go wrong. We just knew we were hot, and we thought pa and ma didn't want us to have any fun. And then, when we'd hardly been in the water any time at all——"

The sobs made Irving's chest ache. And grandpa had his big red handkerchief out, mopping away the tears he shed for a little brother who had been dead more than sixty-five years.

Irving walked over and took the big leather strap down and carried it to his grandfather. "Here, Grandpa," he said, laying it on the table beside him. "I want you to help me to get rid of my besetting sin."

LITTLE THREADER OF NEEDLES, PART I

*T*HE HUNTERS built their camps near beaver meadows and set out long lines of traps for sable, mink, and wildcats. The Indians were everywhere, and it was not unusual to see them at any hour of the day or night. Some of the settlers were afraid of them, but most of the Indians seemed friendly.

In the towns cows wandered along the streets, but some of the leading citizens made laws against having pigs rooting in the main part of town. The town crier came around every time there was a bit of news, and he also came to tell the time of day, for there were no clocks in most homes. People did not particularly need them, for there were few appointments to keep, and no one had to be anywhere at any certain hour. Prayer meeting at the meetinghouse was called at early candlelighting, and the folks walked there with their lanterns made of punched tin, with a candle inside for light.

Not far from where the thriving city of Harrisburg is today, there once stood on the Juniata River a village which the early settlers thought would be a great city someday. But it didn't grow, and the folk who had the dreams are asleep now in one of the old, old graveyards where the graves are sunken and the tombstones are so weather-beaten that you cannot read half the epitaphs. The village was a pretty one, and the log houses stood close to the street, with white board fences in front.

A little girl named Eleanor lived in this pretty village of long ago. Her father was a tailor. America was still a colony that belonged to England, and George III was the king. Eleanor was born in 1770, when radio and television had never been dreamed of. No one could even imagine automobiles. Most important of all for Eleanor, there were no sewing machines. Elias Howe, the man who would dream up the tiny machine that would revolutionize the clothing industry of the world, had not even been born.

The house where Eleanor lived was at the edge of the village, almost at the place where the endless woods began. It was made of split logs and was the biggest house in the village. In the front was a great room called the keeping room. There was a settle by the fireplace, and there were homemade chairs and a homemade table with pewter candlesticks and bowls.

In this room the family spent most of their time. Off

this room were two bedrooms, and to the back in a lean-to was the long kitchen, the most cheerful room in the house. The whole end of the room was full of the fireplace, with a hob and a spit and a brick oven. On the side was a dresser with plates, mugs, and cutlery arranged on the shelves. In the deep-set windows mother had planted flowers—geraniums and baby's tears and live-forever.

But the busy room was off to one side, for it had been added on last. It was the tailor shop. It opened right off the big kitchen. Eleanor was intrigued by this room, for when father was there, it was the most fascinating place in the village. The fireplace at one end was heaped with logs, for father sewed even in the dead of winter, and as he said, a body gets cold from sitting so long in one position. Father liked to sit right in the middle of the big table, cross-legged, and sew. He was proud of the small, even stitches he made.

One day, when Eleanor was only five years old, a man came dashing up to the door of the tailor shop on the back of a great black horse. He jumped down, flung open the door, and stomped into the room. Father was at work on a coat for Deacon Asbury, and was sewing in the satin lining when the man dashed in.

"The colonies are at war with England," he cried. "Word has just come that there have been battles in Massachusetts, at places called Lexington and Concord. Many are dead, but the colonists have won the first fight."

Phineas Baker leaped down from the table, his lean face glowing with excitement. "So," he cried, "the war has come! We have wondered when it would. Some have thought the war was egged on by hotheads, and not necessary at all. But the people are demanding their rights— and you are sure war has really started?"

"Yes, yes, I'm very sure," the young man cried. "The man who came through brought a packet of mail and some papers that described all the fighting. There is a silversmith named Paul Revere, who has a shop in Boston where he makes pots and tea sets and porringers. He went by horseback and warned everyone that the British Regulars were on their way to destroy the powder and stores the colonists had hidden in Lexington. But they had a surprise! The men the silversmith woke up were waiting for the British soldiers. Minutemen, they called them; and there was a battle at the bridge in Concord. Some folks say we are in for a long, hard war. What can we do against such a strong country as England? If only the king had paid attention to some of our complaints!"

"I say so, too. I wish it could have been otherwise. But they say that the time has come to throw caution to the winds," Phineas cried. "We cannot go on being slaves."

"You're right," said the young man. "But that is not what I have come to see you about. You are the tailor, I understand. The people in the next town say you can turn out clothing quicker than anyone else along the river."

Phineas smiled as he lifted the flowered waistcoat on which he was working. "Yes, I think it's true," he said with becoming modesty. "But I would have you know, young man, that I do not sacrifice workmanship for speed."

"That I heard also," declared the young man impatiently. "And that brings me to the business for which I have ridden all these twenty miles up the river; I am going to fight in the war. But before I go, I want to marry my girl and leave her waiting for me. That's the best reason in the world for me to come back alive."

With that, the young man rushed out to his horse and came back carrying a large bundle wrapped in coarse linen.

It was all so exciting that little Eleanor stared almost hypnotized at the young man as he hurriedly unfolded the loosely woven material on the long table where her father had been working.

Undone, the black silk cloth cascaded, shiny and lustrous, over the table. Eleanor was certain that it was the prettiest cloth she had ever seen.

"Where did you get this?" Phineas asked curiously. "It's a beautiful piece of cloth, and I'll warrant it wasn't woven in the mills of New England, or England either."

The young man laughed. "You're right about that," he said. "My uncle came home only last month from the Orient, and he brought it to me from there. He had heard that Letitia and I were promised, and he brought me the cloth for my wedding suit. I have cloth for the waistcoat, too, such as you have never seen."

The smaller roll of silk was so heavy that even Phineas was amazed, and he had seen a lot of cloth in his day. Woven right into it were heavy ridges, and woven into the ridges was what looked like a whole garden of flowers. There was black satin for lining, and white for a shirt and neckcloth, and even reels of special thread to be used for the sewing. Eleanor had never seen the like of it, and neither had her father.

"I want this suit finished by tomorrow night. Yes, and a ruffled shirt as well. Double money for you, and goods for a dress for the little girl here, if it's done on time. But I must have your word that it will be done. I must have it tomorrow night, for I am marrying Letitia Storm day after tomorrow morning, and immediately after, I go to the war."

Phineas had his tape measure out before the young man finished speaking. He called his wife, and she measured for the shirt and the weskit while Phineas was on his knees doing the other measurements. Little Eleanor did nothing but watch, her large blue eyes sparkling with interest.

"You make the shirt and the weskit, and I'll do the rest," Phineas said briskly to his wife. The young man turned suddenly and ran outside. In a moment he returned and laid a roll of cloth in Eleanor's arms. "For you, little one, when you are grown," he said, laughing. "It may be a wedding gown, for it came from China in the hold of a sailing brig, a year to the day on the sea."

While her parents watched, Eleanor carefully opened the roll. It was a purple brocade so lovely that she could hardly believe what she was seeing. She looked up at the rosy-cheeked young man, her pretty eyes shining.

"I shall save it till I'm a young lady. Then maybe someone will love me and will get a black suit and marry me." The young man laughed with delight, and picked serious little Eleanor up and tossed her in the air and kissed her on both of her cheeks.

"Will you help to get my suit ready, little fairy princess?" he asked. "Will you have something to do?"

"Oh, yes," the little girl replied. "I'm the threader of needles. I thread millions and millions of needles, with long tails of thread in them. I'll do that before I go to sleep tonight, so father and mother need not stop sewing, even for a minute."

The young man waved his hand and was off on his fine black horse, up the narrow river road toward the next settlement. No sooner had the door shut behind him than a hum of activity invaded the little shop, for a wedding suit of black silk broadcloth must be made, with a satin weskit and a beautiful pleated and ruffled shirt, all in less than two days.

Eleanor picked up the needle basket and the big pincushion. She went over to the window seat, with two reels of thread, one white and one black. On one side she put the white-threaded needles and on the other, the black. She knew just how long to make the thread, long enough to last awhile and yet not so long that it would knot and get tangled. Her mother brought her another pincushion then, so that she could put the black-threaded needles in one and the white in the other.

Eleanor worked till her fingers ached and her mother told her to run out and play for a while. She got her doll from its trundle bed and ran outside to play in her playhouse by the big maple tree. It was so early in the spring that the crocuses were in bloom along the fence, and the wrinkled noses of the rhubarb stuck up inquisitively through the ground.

She carried her doll out to the fence and looked down the street. The afternoon stage had just arrived, and the post boy would be coming along pretty soon to tell father if he had received any mail from the East. Or perhaps someone would come to give them more news about the war.

War! It was a frightening word. Grandma had told her about wars in Europe when men were killed. Would this be a war like that? Would people she knew get killed?

Then she saw Timothy Byram coming down the street wearing his leather doublet and homespun breeches. He had come from the inn and likely as not had a letter for father. She ran in to tell him, but she got inside just ahead of the big boy.

He had a letter all right. There was no envelope, just a paper folded over and sealed with some red wax and pressed down with a signet ring. There was no stamp on it, so father had to give Timothy a shilling for postage. He laid down his work and opened the letter. It was from Uncle James, who had a store in Boston.

The letter was full of war talk, which interested father, and he kept talking about it off and on all day. Mother wondered if the war would come as far as Pennsylvania. Father thought it probably wouldn't.

"You mark my word, it will be a long, hard war, and will hurt us all," he said grimly. "Who really wants to fight against our mother country? We have cousins and friends over there, and England is in our blood. But it seems there is nothing else we can do."

He went back to sewing then, and little Eleanor went back to threading needles. She tried to keep them threaded as fast as father and mother would finish one and lay down an empty needle, but she had to work fast.

She did not realize that the war beginning in Massachusetts would be a turning point in the history of the world. Not even her mother and father dreamed that a powerful country would grow out of the thirteen colonies.

Father, cross-legged on his table, was sewing frantically. Aunt Patience, who lived down the street and helped when they were in a pinch, was there, too. She padded the ironing table and stood the flatiron up to the fireplace. She was pressing out the pieces of cloth as fast as father and mother got them basted or seamed. When she had finished pressing, she pulled out the white basting threads.

The needle supply was alarmingly low, so Eleanor's small fingers kept busy. Once mother stopped long enough to roll another chunk of wood onto the fire. Uncle Hi, Aunt Patience's husband, helped with the fire, too, and even went to the kitchen and fixed everyone something to eat.

"He's so handy when I'm busy at the loom or the spinning wheel," Aunt Patience said proudly. "I don't think there is another man in the colonies who would pitch in and do for the rest of us the way he does."

In a little bit, Uncle Hi called to tell them that supper

was ready. He had laid the cloth neatly, and there was sassafras tea in the mugs, to be sweetened with maple sugar. There was a dish of Indian pudding that mother had made that morning and some baked pumpkin, and Uncle Hi had made some hoecake, hot and crispy. They all ate, and Uncle Hi told them all to go back to work while he cleaned up the kitchen. So they all went back to the wedding suit. Eleanor began threading needles again. The big folks were working by the light of candles on the table, the drawers, and the mantelpiece. It was not long until little Eleanor was so sleepy that she had to be put to bed. Uncle Hi pulled out the trundle bed, and Aunt Patience helped Eleanor to undress and heard her good-night prayer. The others went back to work again.

All night they worked, and by the afternoon of the next day, the suit was finished, right down to the last button, the last ruffle, the last neat seam. It was pressed, and Aunt Patience was cleaning up the room, mother was putting away the patterns and the needles and the reels of thread, and father was soaking his tired hands in a pan of hot water when the door flew open and the young man came in. His eyes snapped with eagerness.

He went over to the table and feasted his eyes on the beautiful wedding suit. "It is perfect," he said. "I was told you could do it and do it well. I am more than pleased." And Eleanor saw him count out the gold sovereigns for her father. It was more than he had ever gotten for a piece of work before. Then the young man turned and saw Eleanor looking up at him.

"And did you help, my little sugar plum?" he asked.

The little girl nodded her head seriously. "But, sir, I'm sorry. I went to sleep, and Aunt Patience had to put me to bed, so I didn't work all night."

The young man threw back his head and laughed. "But you shall be paid, too," he cried, and out came his money bag again. He took out a huge silver crown piece and pressed it into her small hand. It looked as big as the moon to her, and she was speechless for a moment—but only for a moment. She curtsied as nicely as if she had been four times her age and thanked the young man prettily. It was the first money she had ever had for her very own.

Then the man said, "Mr. Baker, you had better close up your tailor shop and go to war, too. Our soldiers will need uniforms. You can sew fast and well. Men like you will help to keep up the courage of our patriots so that our country can have its freedom."

Phineas looked up quickly. "I have thought of it," he said. "Maybe I will. Maybe I will."

Mother left the room quickly then, for she did not like to hear father talk of going to war. Aunt Patience began to cry.

Eleanor looked curiously at all the big folks. Why were they crying? What was war all about, and why did father think he should go?

LITTLE THREADER
OF NEEDLES,
PART II

*A*BOUT a year after Eleanor had threaded needles to help make the young man's wedding suit, Phineas packed up his shears, his tape measures and needles and other sewing equipment, and went off to join the soldiers who were fighting King George III. Mother cried, and so did Eleanor. It was a terrible thing to see father go away, because he said himself that he had no idea when he would be coming back.

"Maybe a year, maybe two," he told his wife gravely; and Eleanor ran and buried her face in the bright quilt on mother and father's bed when she heard it. A year was such a long time. Why, it was more than a year since the young man had come to have his wedding suit made, and that seemed like a lifetime ago. But father had already packed his clothes and put them in the saddlebags on Old Roan, the horse he was going to ride.

"I'll write to you, Becky," he told his wife. "And you be a good girl, Ellie," he said, calling her by her baby name.

Eleanor and mother stood on the doorstep and watched him till he rode out of sight on the forest path. He turned at the last and waved his hand in a final farewell.

It was four years before they saw father. Then he came home for only a few days and left again. When the war was finally over, Eleanor was nearly twelve years old. It seemed to her like a hundred years since father had used the tailor shop.

One winter day Eleanor saw what she thought was an old, old man hobbling up the path. They were having the first bad November cold snap, and the weather had been below zero for several days. Suddenly Eleanor screamed. The old man was her father!

Eleanor ran like lightning to meet him. He was almost beyond help. He hardly knew his own daughter. She half dragged, half carried him into the house and put him to bed. She and mother thawed out his feet with cold water, but it was not possible to save them. Gangrene soon set in, and poor father, who loved to walk and climb mountains and wade through brooks, had to have his feet cut off. That was long before anyone knew about ether or chloroform, so the painful operation was done without an anesthetic. Eleanor had to run to the barn and hide in the stall with the old driving horse and cry while it happened.

When father began to get better, he had some tales to tell.

"After Cornwallis surrendered," he told the family, "we thought we would be out of the army before winter, but then I got orders to go to New York.

"You ought to see New York," he exclaimed. His face was tan and weather-beaten against the snow-white pillowcase. "I saw the place where Nathan Hale died. They say that one of the soldiers jeered at him for having to be hanged. 'Fine death for a soldier to die,' he said to Nathan. 'I only regret,' Nathan answered, 'that I have but one life to give for my country.' My, I liked that. I went up to Third Avenue many a time to see the spot where the British strung him up. He was a great American."

Then father told them that there was still fighting going on in New York when he started for home. He and a man from near Philadelphia started traveling together, but the woods were so thick that they got lost more times than they could count.

"Then it turned so cold that we nearly froze one night. We couldn't find a cabin, and we needed one. We had camped out Indian fashion before, putting up boughs like a wigwam and piling leaves around them. We got along all right that way until it got so cold. We couldn't get a fire started, and we both froze our feet. I went to the creek to get mine thawed. I broke a hole in the ice and put them down in the water with my shoes on. But since we didn't have a fire, we only froze our feet again when we took them out."

Father got well, but the stumps of his legs were tender for a long time. After a while he made some pads for the stumps at the ends of his ankles and got around amazingly well. Eleanor was proud of him.

George Sewall, one of the local boys, came courting Eleanor, and father made up the lovely purple dress for her. Because great mushroom hoop skirts were the style, he made the skirt with ten widths of cloth in it. It was 360 inches around. For once, her mother disapproved. "You're spoiling that girl," she sniffed. "Whoever heard of a dress with thirty feet of cloth around the bottom?"

After Eleanor and George were married, the years spun by so fast that it was hard for Eleanor to believe that a year had seemed so long when she was a little girl.

By the time she was twenty-five Eleanor had four children. The oldest one was a girl named Julia, frail and lovely as a pearl. The other three were boys. Suddenly the family decided to move from Pennsylvania to a state so far away that it seemed like a foreign country—Indiana. They had to get there by sailing down the Ohio River in a boat, taking all their household goods with them. Eleanor's mother and father wept at their going, and George told them they had better come along.

"No," said Phineas. "My roots are down here, and I'll stay till I die."

He did, too. Eleanor never saw him or her mother again, though they sent her a picture once that father had taken on a new contraption called an ambrotype. Eleanor had to hold it in the light and look at it by turning it this

way and that to see who it was. Her father looked so old
and feeble she could hardly believe it was really he.

George and Eleanor settled near a small town in central Indiana called Russiaville. George got a big farm, and
they homesteaded it. Then, as if the years were playing a
game of hide-and-seek, Julia grew up, got married, and
moved to a store in town where her young husband, Will
Thomas, sold nails, cheese, lamp oil, calico, and a hundred
other necessities.

In 1848 a very unusual thing happened. Eleanor was
seventy-eight years old then. George had died the year
before, and she lived with her son Jackson, who was a
doctor. Two strange young men came to Russiaville. They
started holding meetings in the biggest church in the town,
and even that church could not hold the crowds. It was
unbelievable. Men put up sawhorses and stood at the
church windows so that they could see and hear the boy
preacher, Moses Hull.

Eleanor wore her old sunbonnet to the church every
night. In those days people did not have all the pretty
clothes that we have now, but Eleanor's sunbonnet was a
thing of beauty. It had wooden stays in it to keep it stiff,
and she wore it with the air of a queen. She wore the
paisley shawl that Phineas, her father, had given her. It
was sixty years old if it was a day.

For the first time Eleanor learned that the world was
going to come to an end. She heard the preacher read from
the Bible that the Lord Jesus, who came to the world as a
babe in Bethlehem, had promised to return. The prophe-

cies were as plain as day. Before long the whole world would be plunged into a time of war and trouble. The Bible said so.

Finally, Moses Hull revealed a most amazing thing. It seemed that Eleanor had never kept the real Sabbath of the Lord. Never had! She could hardly believe that, for she had tried as long as she lived to do as little as possible on Sunday, and always go to church and keep the day holy. Now the preacher told her she couldn't keep it holy, for it had never been a holy day in the first place. It was all bewildering to a woman almost eighty years old.

Julia and her husband were delighted with the things they were learning at the meetings. They invited Mr. Hull to their house as often as they could.

Always after Eleanor got home from the meetings, she would sit in her rocking chair and smoke at least two pipefuls of tobacco while she pondered the things she had heard. She had begun to smoke a pipe after she had come to the Indiana Territory, for she seemed to have asthma. A doctor told her that there was no remedy so good as a pipeful of tobacco to warm up the lungs and the throat. So Eleanor acquired the habit. She smoked a pipeful after breakfast and one after dinner, and when she had a cup of tea in the afternoon, she had another pipeful.

Once her son, Dr. Sewall, told her, "Mother, I wonder if we won't find out someday that the cure of asthma with tobacco is worse than the disease. I can't see that it is helping you any."

But Eleanor was on the defensive. "Oh, yes it does,

Jackson," she said. "I just feel myself getting all calmed down when I puff. I know it must be good."

But Eleanor started to worry just the same. She had never seen Elder Hull smoking. She wondered if folks would chew tobacco in heaven and spit all over the golden streets. She wondered if she would have a cob pipe, and if she would have to sit down every little bit all day and smoke it.

At first she liked to read in her Bible while she was puffing. But after a while she stopped doing that. She liked so much to read about the home the Lord was preparing in heaven. She read about the pure river of life, clear as crystal. At that thought she remembered that a few days before, when she and Julia had gone to town, they were walking over the bridge across Wildcat Creek. She saw a man standing there chewing, and he spat a long stream of tobacco juice straight into the creek. Suddenly, she thought of the river of life. How long would it stay as clear as crystal if the saved of all nations were spitting brown tobacco juice into it? She got so worried about it that she went and put her pipe away.

One night the sermon was about the great judgment day. Elder Hull said that every secret thing, good and evil, would be brought into judgment—*everything*. Everything we love better than we love God. Every useless indulgence, for no one can take such things into heaven.

Old Eleanor thought of the corncob pipe she loved so much. She would rather sit down with that pipe than have a piece of cake. She would rather have the pipe than eat. She got more hungry for tobacco than she did for food. All of her apron pockets were full of the leaves she chafed in her hands to stuff into the pipe. She almost lived for it.

Poor Eleanor went home that night very unhappy. She automatically went to get her pipe, as she had always done. Then she stopped and thought, "Maybe I will not have my pipeful tonight. I'll go to bed without it." But she seemed not to be able to do without it. She tried to undress, but she couldn't quit thinking about the pipe. Finally she went and got it and had her smoke. But she told herself that she would have only one, not two, and tomorrow she would be stronger and have none at all.

She went to bed, but it was a long time before she could get to sleep. Suddenly she was having a dream. It seemed that Jesus had come, and she was going to heaven with Him. All the way to heaven on the cloud she felt bad because she had forgotten to take her pipe, and she wondered what she was going to do without it.

Finally the gates of pearl came in sight. Right by the gate was a lovely angel with the biggest book she had ever seen. He was talking to everyone and looking up his record before he could enter the glorious city. Finally her turn came.

"My name is Eleanor Sewall. I used to be Eleanor Baker, and I lived in Pennsylvania. Now I live in Indiana," she told the angel.

"Yes," the angel said in the loveliest voice she had ever heard. "Yes, you have been living in Indiana. But if you can qualify—if I find your name in the book of life—you will live with Jesus forever here in the New Jerusalem."

"I'm sure I can qualify," Eleanor declared. "I believed. I began to keep the Sabbath of the Lord. I began getting ready for His coming as soon as I learned of it. I——"

"If this is all true," the angel said, "you have nothing to worry about. Your name will be here. But, Eleanor, I cannot find it. I'm looking right where it should be, but it is not here."

"Look!" screamed Eleanor, suddenly wild with agony. "Look again! It must be there! It *has* to be there! I did not miss one night of the Hull and Wagner meetings. And we all accepted what they said. We did, I tell you."

"Be patient," said the angel kindly. "If your name is here, you can go right in. But, Eleanor, I just don't see your name. Here's a name that I cannot read at all, it is so blurred and blotched with smoke. It smells like tobacco smoke to me. There can be nothing filthy in heaven, Eleanor."

Eleanor cried aloud and woke herself up. Her daughter-in-law, Waitstill, was knocking on her door.

"What's the matter, Mother?" she cried. "Let me in. You must be sick."

Eleanor got up and unlocked the door. "Oh, Waity," she moaned. "I was crying. I dreamed that Jesus came, and I was not saved. And all because of tobacco, Waity. The angel couldn't find my name because it was so blurred with tobacco smoke. I'm going to quit, Waity. I'm going to quit."

"Oh, Mother, can you? You've used tobacco for so many years!"

Eleanor lifted her head proudly. "Of course I can." She spoke firmly. "The Bible says, 'I can do all things through Christ which strengtheneth me.'"

Eleanor did stop her smoking. Before the meetings were over, she accepted all the other points of Bible truth, and Elder Hull baptized her. When she came up out of the water that day, her face shone with a great smile of victory and happiness.

When Eleanor was a little girl, it seemed the biggest thing in her life was threading needles to help make the wedding suit for the young man who was getting married. Now she knew that something much more important had happened to her. Now she had received from Christ the most beautiful clothing anyone can ever wear—the righteousness of Christ. Wearing that robe of righteousness, she could walk the streets of gold and drink the water of the river of life and attend the wedding of the Lamb of God.

WHAT SHALL I DO WITH MY LIFE?

A BOY your age ought t' know where he's goin' and what he wants to do with his life," Uncle Si said suddenly.

The family were all sitting around the fire in the living room except mother, who was straightening up the kitchen and the dining room, washing dishes, sweeping the floor, and polishing the stove.

It was cold outside, and the wind whipped around the corner of the house with angry snarls, as if it resented the storm windows and the tight weather stripping that kept it out of the cozy house.

John looked around the warm, comfortable room, half seeing it, and only half hearing his uncle's remark. Before supper Uncle Si had asked him point-blank what he wanted to be when he "set out in life," and John had pretended he didn't know yet. He had sort of shaken his head and tried to put him off. But that was hard to do, for Uncle Si was a persistent soul.

They had gone in to supper then, and Uncle Si got interested in the savory smells and the loaded table. Mother was a famous cook and could do more with her mixing bowl, breadboard, rolling pin, and her big black coal-and-wood stove than anyone else in town.

Uncle Si had piled the crispy corn fritters on his plate and slathered them with butter. He poured on maple syrup till the plate looked like an amber lake. If they had not had their own maple grove and made their own syrup, Uncle Si's eating habits might have been expensive.

Once away from the table, Uncle Si took up the subject again. "Now, you could be a farmer, just like your pa," he speculated, picking his teeth with a wooden splinter. He reared back in his chair and hooked one heel over a rung and swung the other. "This is a good farm. Your pa needs you bad. With times as hard as they are, an extry pair of hands would be a mighty big help."

When John didn't answer, Pa spoke up.

"With these hard times, Si, there ain't nothin' in farmin'. Of course, we've got plenty to eat, which is a lot more than folks in town have. I don't see how they get along, myself. Food ain't a problem to us; but shoes, books, and stamps, and things we can't raise, are something else. I feel sorry for John here. He'd ought to have better clothes, goin' to high school, but we do the best we can."

"You do all right, Dad," John said quietly. "I guess we aren't the only family having a hard time right now."

Then John turned to his uncle. "I've been thinking about several different things, Uncle Si," he said. "It just isn't easy to get into anything, but times are bound to get better. Everyone says so."

Then father and Uncle Si began to talk about what Hitler was doing in Europe, and the possibility of war. The year was 1940, and World War II had already begun in Europe, though America wasn't in it yet. "It's always easier to make money when there's a war," father said. "But I don't like to get rich that way."

John went back to his own thoughts and dreams and let father and Uncle Si speculate on what President Roosevelt was going to do, and whether the lend-lease idea was a good thing. How could he tell Uncle Si what he really wanted to do? He would never understand. He had never gone to high school. Dad and mother and Uncle Si and even grandma talked a lot about the one-room schoolhouse on the four corners, where they had gone to school. They often talked of ciphering all over the blackboard and getting the prize in spelling.

"Teachers nowadays would have to get up early in the mornin' and dust their britches to know more'n old man Hazel. He learned us everythin' from spellin' to history. My! he knowed that arithmetic book from kiver to kiver!" Uncle Si chuckled a long time, remembering. John looked at him and wondered just how much grammar the remarkable Mr. Hazel had taught in the crowded school.

But really, dad and Uncle Si had done well with what they had. They had played baseball down in the pasture for fun. And in the schoolyard, they had played "scrub" and "work-up." What would Uncle Si say if he knew John had his mind set on really big things?

About a month before, something had happened to change John's whole way of thinking. He had pitched when Singerman High played baseball against Orton, and the crowd had gone wild more than once, watching his brilliant plays and his home runs. After the game he had seen a strange man talking to the coach, and they were both looking in his direction.

Later, Coach Watts called him in. "That was a scout for the big league, John," he had said with pride in his eyes. "I think you've got it made, boy." He laid his hand on John's shoulder. "That man said you're the best prospect he has found for professional playing. He took your name and address, and he'll get in touch with you. Salaries for professional ballplayers make a farm income look silly, John. Singerman High will be proud of you."

He had gone home, his head in a spin. At first he could hardly wait to tell the folks. But after thinking it over, he decided to do as the coach suggested, and tell no one.

"Be better to surprise folks and then brag, than brag too soon," the older man had suggested.

So John said nothing, though he almost burst. After that he had thrown himself into practice with every speck of energy he had. He got his lessons as quickly as he could and learned to budget his time.

"I won't let my grades get low," he thought. "I still want to graduate with honors. But boy, I sure am lucky! I guess my future is really laid out for me!" And off he would run to a vacant lot to practice pitching and catching, and to bat with the boys. He was completely consumed with his ambition.

John knew what would happen if he told father and Uncle Si that he wanted to be a professional ballplayer. Father would look bewildered, and Uncle Si would holler, "So *you* think you could get into that big-time stuff, huh? You? Listen, Johnny, be realistic. Ain't one man in ten thousand gets a chance, and when they do, they hafta have pull, which you ain't got. Better come down to earth and decide to work for a living instead of playing all your life."

Then dad, half understanding, would probably say, "John, I know you like to play baseball better than you like cake and ice cream. But don't set your heart on something like that. I haven't known much but hard work, and I'm afraid that's what's facing you. It's a good life, son. Work is a man's friend."

Of course, father and Uncle Si had not gone to high school, nor did either one of them know much about the big leagues and professional baseball. They couldn't know the feeling that comes over a boy when he hears the bat go *clink*, sees the ball sail high over the fielders' heads, and tears around the bases for a home run. The prettiest girls, and everyone else in the grandstands, would yell themselves hoarse: "Go! Go! Johnny, old boy! Yea, Johnny!" No, they couldn't know. They had never tasted victory and applause, loud-spoken admiration and half-crazy crowds. He would just have to show them what he could do before they would understand.

That year, about midterm, a boy came to high school from the north end of the state. His folks had moved to town. John didn't understand the new boy, though he was strangely attracted to him. He was tall, quiet, and studious. His name was Fred Lyons, and that soon became almost a synonym for straight A grades. Some of the boys, better at excuses than they were at studying, would make fun of him. They'd say, "At least we're not ferocious. We don't go to classes like Lyons."

Big, tall Fred took their jibes good-naturedly. He would grin a little, then go into the library, and would soon be deep in some book or other. One day John sat down beside Fred in the library.

"What're you reading?" he whispered, pulling up his chair.

Fred lifted up the cover of the book and showed John the title: *Napoleon,* by Emil Ludwig.

"For what class?" John leaned closer, for the librarian was very strict about talking in the library.

Fred took a piece of paper and wrote in a heavy, neat hand, "None. I just like to read."

John thought about that for a while. Reading history or biography for pleasure was something he had just not met up with very often. He looked at Fred curiously. Most of the boys complained bitterly about teachers who assigned too much outside reading. "Who wants to read books?" they'd say. "What does she think we are? The old crab!"

John had been attracted to Fred mostly because he was different from the crowd. He was clean-cut, quiet, and didn't seem to mind that he was very often alone.

Suddenly John was curious. Fred was big and strong. John could see his muscles rippling under his neatly ironed shirt. With his strong arms and long legs, why in the world hadn't he tried out for the baseball team? He leaned closer.

"Comin' to the game Friday night?" he queried.

Fred looked up briefly, a half smile on his face. He shook his head. "Can't," he whispered. Then, as if to qualify what he had just said, he added, "And I really don't want to, either."

John could hardly believe that. What kind of answer was that? Why would a guy like Fred not want to go to a ball game. He decided to find out more about this.

After school John got into his jalopy. He saw Fred walking along the sidewalk with half a dozen books under his arm, reading as he walked. John honked, and Fred looked up.

"Wanna lift?" John asked.

"No, I'm home already," Fred said, and jerked his thumb toward a neat cottage back in the trees. "Come in a minute, if you want to."

John was so curious that he flipped off the ignition and brought the car to a stop, scraping the curb with both wheels. He climbed out.

"I can't stay long. Gotta get home and do chores. I live half a mile out Cornbread Road. I usually walk. Gas comes too high to drive all the time. My folks aren't rich."

"I know what you're talking about," Fred agreed. "We've had a lot of bad luck since my father got hurt. That's why we moved here, to be near the hospital."

"That's tough," John said. "Where did you go to school before you came here?"

"I was in a boarding school, an academy. Mom didn't want me to leave—this was my fourth year there—but I had to, to help her with dad. I'll graduate anyway, and I'm glad I didn't lose any credits."

That day started a strange friendship that John was drawn into almost in spite of himself. Fred's little house was very clean and attractive. Red geraniums bloomed in the windows. Big braided rugs covered the floor. There were books everywhere—in big bookcases, on tables, and on chair arms. Fred's father was recovering from a terrible accident he had had on a logging job. He greeted John kindly, and so did Fred's mother, a tall woman with black hair and blue eyes. Every line of her face seemed to be set in sweetness.

"How have you been today, Dad?" Fred asked and went over and kissed the man in the wheelchair.

He smiled and patted Fred's hand. "Quite a bit better, son. I don't think it will be long until I can be walking. I'll be so glad."

"So will we, Dad."

It was plain to be seen that the little family was having

a hard time, and John resolved to speak to his parents about them. His own family were in dire straits as far as money was concerned, but they had worlds of food—eggs, butter, cottage cheese, milk, and buttermilk. And there were enough potatoes and apples in the cellar to supply an army.

Fred had a job at a local grain elevator. He worked afternoons and all day Sunday. Now he hurried to his room to change his clothes. John went with him.

"Sorry to rush, John, but I have to get ready for work."

"I know," John said. "I'll drive you."

"Boy, thanks. I am a little late."

When John got home, he told his folks about Fred's family. Uncle Si had a lot to say.

"Yes, I know them," he said. "He's a good fellow, not a lazy bone in his body, and almost crazy honest. Back during the war—1917, 1918—we was in the same outfit, afore we was shipped overseas. One day the grocery company made a mistake and doubled the order fer the commissary shack. There was a lot more stuff than we could eat before it spoiled. Most of the fellows took a lot of it home with them. Carl Lyons—why he wouldn't touch a thing. ' 'Tain't mine,' he said. 'An' I won't take a thing less'n it's give to me or I buy it.' "

"He was right," John's father said emphatically. "There's too much free an' easy takin' in a place like that. I could trust a man like Carl Lyons, if that's the way he does."

"Ye-e-e-e-s." Uncle Si rumpled his bushy hair speculatively. "But you kin run things like that in the ground, I'd

say. 'Nother thing. Carl Lyons wouldn't work Saturday fer
no one.''

John looked up.

"Saturday!" he exclaimed. "You mean Sunday, don't
you?"

"No, I don't. I mean Saturday. That's the day they
keep fer Sunday. I told him it was an old Jew day, but he
argued with me, and told me it was for everyone, and it
had never been changed by God, even though people had
tried to do a lot of things to God's law. A lot of the guys
argued with him, but he got the best of all of us. As fer
me, I don't know much about the Bible, not enough to
speak of."

Uncle Si leaned his chair back by the fireplace and
sat there, his eyes half shut, thinking over what he had
just said.

" 'Nother thing, John. He told me that the Catholic
Church had changed the day from Saturday to Sunday.
He says they laugh up their sleeves at Protestants fer
pretendin' to be agin the Catholic Church, when they
ain't really protestin' at nothin'. That got me half mad,
but I didn't say nothin'. Didn't know nothin' to say."

Grandma Piper looked up from her mending. She was
putting a neat patch on an overall leg, setting it on with
precise, microscopic stitches.

"You wouldn't have," she observed. "There wouldn't
be anything to say if what he says is true."

"Oh, I reckon it is, all right. Carl Lyons usually
knowed what he was talking about. Didn't say nothing he

couldn't prove. Didn't pay to argue too much with him."

John, thinking of Fred and his sometimes unusual ways, was suddenly even more curious.

"Uncle Si," he asked, "did you ever find out anything about Friday night from Mr. Lyons? Fred won't go to the ball games on Friday night. Once he said he didn't even want to."

"Oh, that——" Uncle Si let the legs of the chair plop down on the floor. "Now, that is right in the Bible. Carl read it to me. And for that matter, we got good proof of it in the way Christmas begins. It starts on Christmas Eve, you all know that. Carl says that Catholics changed that, too. Days really begin at sundown, he said, not at midnight. They begin their Sabbath day on Friday night at sunset."

John turned this over in his mind. So that was it. Well, Fred must like it, if he didn't even want to go to the game.

Then John really began to wonder what kind of religion could get hold of a boy as young as Fred. Why, himself, he did not even care about going to church. He only went because his mother wanted him to.

One night when the boys were walking home from school, Fred told John that he was going to visit the college he planned to attend when he got through high school. He had a chance to go the next day, which was Friday.

"Dad's well now," he said, "and I'll be going there to school next year. Tomorrow I want to see about some work they promised me for the summer. They have a woodshop, and they said I'd probably be able to work there. My Aunt

Jean is driving up, and she's taking me. I'll get to stay all weekend."

"Oh, are you going to college?"

"Why, of course," Fred answered, in a tone that made John know there had never been any question about it. "I have to go to college, since I'm going to be a minister."

"A minister!" John exclaimed.

"Oh, yes," Fred replied. "I think I have always wanted to be a minister. I guess that's why I like to read so well. Ministers ought to know a great many things, so that their sermons will be interesting and helpful."

"I can agree with you there," John said emphatically, remembering some of the dry sermons he had heard. "But I don't see how you can *want* to be a minister. It doesn't sound very exciting."

"It is, though. My uncle went to the South Seas as a missionary. If you want to hear something exciting, listen to him talk. I think just helping people can be kind of exciting. As far as I'm concerned, I think it's funny for anyone to just want to be nothing."

"Well, I guess you have something there," John said with a laugh. "I suppose not more than one or two of us graduates have any plans. When school is out this spring, I have no idea whether what I want to do will pan out or not. I haven't told anyone, but I may have a chance to do something really great. The coach told me I'm to get to try out for big-league baseball. A scout saw me play and took my name. I'll get the date of my tryout any day now."

He glanced at Fred, expecting a look of admiration and

envy and disbelief. But he didn't see it. Instead, Fred shook his head.

"You said you didn't see how anyone could want to be a minister or a missionary. Well, I don't see how anyone could possibly want to be a professional ballplayer. I think it would be as it was when I went to see my Uncle Philip, who owns a candy store. I thought how wonderful it would be to eat all the candy in the store. Uncle Philip let me have all I could hold, and in two days I was wishing I was back home with mother's homemade bread and butter."

John was disappointed. Most of the boys at the high school would have been goggle-eyed. They would have shouted, "The big league! Man! Are you in luck!"

But Fred simply said, "I suppose I should congratulate you, John. I'm glad you're getting the chance, if that is what you want to do with your life."

On the way home, John turned the matter over in his mind. "If that's what you want to do with your life." He kept remembering those words. The way Fred had said it, John knew he did not think being a professional ballplayer was the fantastic thing John had always thought it was. He began to suspect that there were heights to reach that he had never thought of before.

When John got home that night, dad was all excited. "Here's a letter for you, son," he said, and his voice was actually shaking. John did not know, but the coach had called dad up and told him about the opportunity John was about to have. Dad held out the long envelope. "It looks important."

John tore it open. It was all he had hoped for, even in his wildest dreams. It was the chance he had never thought he would have. The scout had recommended him so highly that the letter said he would have a perfect chance to go straight to the top. He was to come for an interview and a tryout. The school had given permission for him to be absent for a couple of days. He was to check in at the Palace Hotel.

John's head began to buzz, it was all so important and grand. Then, when he went to his room, a strange doubt nagged at his mind. Was that really what he wanted to do with his life?

The doorbell rang. John laid down the letter and went to answer it. Fred was there, bubbling with excitement. He grabbed John's arm.

"John, go and ask your folks if you can come with me to the college tomorrow. Aunt Jean says she can take you, if you want to go. I like the college so much, and I would love for you to see where I will be next year. Aunt Jean has already made arrangements for us to stay in the dorm. We'll be back Sunday afternoon."

Suddenly John wanted to go with Fred worse than anything. Fred had given him a glimpse of a life he had not dreamed existed. John had been bounded by the narrow confines of a small town and a small farm. He had been surrounded by people who had not accomplished much and who had not given him the challenge to do much better. He wanted to talk with Fred about the uneasy feeling he had about making baseball his career.

John enjoyed that weekend in spite of himself. He liked the orderly politeness in the dining room. The church service was entirely different from what he had been accustomed to. There were no groups of boys standing around making unsavory remarks. No one was smoking. The teachers were friendly and kind. He went into the woodshop while the superintendent was interviewing Fred. The man turned to John and asked, "Do you want a job, too?"

He hesitated only an instant. Then he answered, "Do you think I could earn most of my way? My parents can't help me much."

The superintendent looked him straight in the eye. "That will depend on you, young man. If you're a good worker, you can do it. If you have to be watched and checked on all the time, you can't. It will be strictly up to you."

All of a sudden John knew what he wanted to do with his life. He wanted to climb higher than the big league. He would have to go to college!

That summer the two boys worked together, and while they did, John learned to love the wonderful truth of the Bible. He went home every once in a while with a Bible in his suitcase. Even Uncle Si was impressed and crowded into the living room when John began explaining texts to the family. John heard Uncle Si talking to Grandma Piper once. He was telling her, "I figger John will be something perty big. He knows the Bible better'n anyone I've ever heard."

John and Fred are both ministers now. And Uncle Si did so much missionary work in the church after he was baptized that they made him the missionary leader. Every time John hears a ball game on the radio or watches the World Series on TV, he is glad he decided what he really wanted to do with his life.

CAUGHT BY
THE SLAVERS

*T*HE STORY of Christianity had never been heard in the little village far to the south of Nyasaland, Africa. There were other stories, though, that the old people told as they sat around the leaping fires at night. It was then that the old village grandfather came into his own. If he was a good storyteller, he was popular with everyone.

Children clung close to their mothers' arms when his tales got frightening. He told of charging buffalo, roaring lions, and of the cowardly hyena, who attacked only little children, or someone old, weak, or sick.

But the stories that made Kanena shiver the most were the tales of the terrible slavers. Kanena kept his eyes on his father's strong face and deep-set eyes when old Kathamanga told of the days of his childhood.

"A village sat right there on that hill where the sugar-cane is planted." The old man pointed a crooked, gnarled finger toward the tasseled cane, waving limber arms against the evening sky.

Kanena tried to imagine a village there, with paths and houses and grain bins, and people walking between the huts.

"My mother," Kathamanga continued, "had made us porridge that night, and we were gathered around the pot, eating. Suddenly the slavers came at us with flaring torches, guns, and spears. I ran and hid in the jungle. I never saw a single one of my family again.

"It was terrible," the old man reminisced. "We were eating, and everything was peaceful and quiet. Then suddenly everyone was screaming, shouting. Well, as I told you, I ran into the jungle and climbed up into that old tree there."

Kanena looked where the grandfather was pointing. He saw a gnarled old mahogany tree, its trunk so fat and thick that the boy wondered how anyone could possibly climb it.

It was almost as though the grandfather heard his thoughts. "Maybe you wonder how I climbed that big tree. Well, it wasn't as big sixty-five or seventy years ago. But even so, I skinned right up that tree trunk like a lizard. It's surprising what you can do when you have to."

Again Kanena looked at the face of Lyson, his father. He was glad that those days of fear and slavery were gone, never to return—he thought.

"What did you do then, Kathamanga?" someone was always bound to ask, even though they knew his story by heart. The old man would sometimes stop, deep in thought, and forget to go on unless someone reminded him.

He lifted his grizzled old head in surprise. "Oh, yes," he said. "I forgot. Well, I stayed up in that tree all night and all the next day. The slavers burned the village to the ground. In the night hyenas came up and licked up the food that we'd left in the pot.

"I came down out of the tree the next night and slept on top of the corn in the high granary, so as to be safe from the animals. I woke up once, and a rat had chewed the callouses on the heel of my left foot till he brought blood."

Kanena knew what that meant. He had been awakened many a night by a rat that bit too deep.

One day soon after that, Kanena's father went hunting and didn't come back. Gossip had gone around the villages that a great world war was raging on the other side of the world. White men were making bigger wars and killing more people than could be done with the bow and arrow. They had great fire-throwing logs that could wreck whole villages with one shot, and guns that could find an enemy's heart many paces away.

Lyson was probably thinking about the great war as he crossed the small stream at the base of the hill and walked through the jungle toward a valley where small deer were often seen. Here he hoped to find food to take home to his wife and children. He had no gun, but he did have a small skin holder full of arrows, and a huge bow.

Little Kanena was about six when his father left to hunt for that deer. He was sixteen when his father returned. The baby girl Lyson left behind had been dead for more than six years, and Cuichi, Kanena's brother, had been drowned when the river flooded. Only Kanena and his mother were left when the stranger came into the village, slowly, hesitantly, one evening near nightfall.

But Kanena's mother knew her husband. She leaped up from the mat with a loud cry. "My Lyson! Where have you been all these long years?"

That night, as the flames of the village fire burned low, Kanena heard a story that truly astonished him. For Lyson, his own father, had been captured by slavers.

"As I was kneeling and taking careful aim at the deer with my bow and arrow," Lyson began, "fierce men seized and bound me."

Who these men were he had no idea. But they forced him to march for many days till they came to a vast plantation where sisal was grown for ropes and mats.

Here, with many other slaves, Lyson labored under a boiling sun long hours every day. At night the men were locked in a strong building with bars on the windows and heavy locks on the doors.

Lyson dreamed constantly of his village and his wife and children as he labored with hoe and reaping knife by day and tried to sleep in the suffocating heat of the stronghold at night.

"Why didn't you try to escape?" asked Kanena quietly, watching the thin, scarred face of his father.

A fleeting expression of agony clouded his father's eyes. "I saw others who tried and failed," he said simply. "Death is better than what those men got. I laid my plans carefully. Even if it took years, I said I would not try to escape till I knew I could do it. Now, at last, I'm here," he added.

"Did it take you long to find your way back?" asked one of the villagers.

"It took me as many days as I have toes and fingers, with one more hand besides. I started walking every day from the rising of the sun. Finally one morning I saw the two mountains our fathers called Chiperoni and Nakumbi. Then I knew that I was near to the land of my fathers."

After his escape from the slavers, Lyson lived long enough to hear about Jesus, and he accepted Christianity and was baptized. And Kanena, his son, was baptized at the same time.

Lyson saw Kanena start to school and with great pleasure heard him learn to read. Finally Kanena went away to a bigger school to learn to be a teacher. While he was gone, Lyson died of malaria.

The custom in Africa is for friends and family to return to the village and "see where they laid the loved one." In that hot climate they bury the dead the same day they die, so it isn't possible to wait for people to come to the funeral.

When Kanena got home, his mother led him to the cemetery. A broken pot, made white with powdered limestone, marked the place where Lyson lay.

As Kanena stood there, he looked into his mother's sad

face and told her something that has made people glad all over the world.

"Lyson, my father," he said, "will live again when Jesus comes!" And Kanena was glad, too, that his father would awake in a glad, free world, where all men would be happy and filled with love for one another.

MASTER SIDWALA AND THE ROARING LION

*I*N FARAWAY Africa, in a small village in Nyasaland, a little boy was born about forty years ago. Since his father and his mother were Christians, it looked as though little Master, as Samuel and Elizabeth Sidwala called their son, would have a good life ahead of him.

But Nyasaland is an unhealthful country, even though it looks beautiful on the surface. Malaria sleeps in everybody's veins, and the deadly mosquitoes rise from the jungle in great clouds every night. The people suffer from many strange and deadly diseases.

When Master was just a tiny little boy, his mother died. He trotted in and out of the hut where she lay on a mat on the floor and didn't understand in the least what was happening. He did not cry at first, for he did not know what death was. But he cried hard when night came, because he usually slept by his mother, and now she was gone. His father took him onto his mat and tried to comfort him, but he couldn't help much because he was sick, too. His thin body was hot with fever.

A few days later, Master's father died also. Now the little boy was all alone. After his father's funeral, his wrinkled grandparents came from their heathen village and took little Master Sidwala home with them. He was too young to realize that this could mean disaster for him, because his grandparents' heathen minds were full of superstition and ignorance.

In the hut of these old ones was a hideous carved idol that his grandparents called Chikhaliro. They worshiped this ugly piece of discolored wood and kept affirming every time they prayed that they were in this world because Chikhaliro looked after them and protected them from harm.

When they needed rain, or when sickness plagued the village, or when some trouble came up, the old grandpa always killed a chicken and roasted the liver over the hot coals. Then he offered this in sacrifice to the splintered old idol.

He would lay it out in front of the idol and pray in a loud voice for Chikhaliro to have mercy and watch over them. They were very sure that Master's parents had died because they had stopped trusting in this old idol and had gone off to serve a new God instead. This was very obvious to their simple heathen minds.

Right in this heathen village was a small, very poor school. Even though the old grandparents thought that learning was pure nonsense, they didn't say much or bother their old heads any when Master Sidwala went to school. What difference could it make?

One day Master came home and read some very strange things to them from marks on a piece of paper. The old man took the paper and looked at it closely. How could the boy say that these scratches meant "dog" or "children" or even "grandfather"? He couldn't see a thing but some lines and circles. It was witchcraft, he declared.

A few days later, the child brought home what he called a book, and read to his grandparents some stories from the Bible. The old people were filled with amazement and pride that this small lizard of a boy could do things that even they could not do. And because they were proud of him, they didn't object when he wanted to go to another school. He had learned everything that the two grades in the small village school could teach him.

When the time came for school to open, several people went with small Master Sidwala to the village of his Uncle Mankwala, his father's oldest brother. It would have been very dangerous for him to go alone, for the jungle was full of wild animals.

When his new school opened, bright little Master sat on the very front row. The bigger boys, who were mainly interested in having a good time, asked him why he was sitting there. He said, "Because I have come to school to learn. I want to be a great one." When they saw it was useless to try to get him involved in any of their escapades, they let him alone.

His school was just a long mud building, thatched with grass and floored with mud. The seats were homemade bricks piled up and plastered over with mud. There was no glass in the windows nor any door in the doorway.

Master didn't criticize the school, for he had never seen anything better. He didn't mind that he had to practice his writing with a sharp stick on the smooth ground. Everyone was too poor to own pencils and paper.

But the thing that made Master the happiest was that his Uncle Mankwala and his Aunt Idesi were Christians. They did not have an idol like Chikhaliro, as his grandparents had.

"My boy," his uncle said kindly, "we will teach you in the way of Christ, the way your parents would have taught you."

At their home, Master learned what it means to be a Christian, and he started going to church. He learned to pray to the same God his father and mother had worshiped, and that made him very happy.

Then a terrible thing happened. One day while Master and the other children were at school, a lion got into the herd of cattle belonging to the villagers. He was a rough, fierce, old fellow, and he struck down and killed a fine bull.

Mankwala was a brave man. He called all the village men together and told them of the danger which threatened them.

"The lion will endanger the whole village," he said quietly. "No one will dare to go to the creek, to the jungle, or to the garden. We must try to drive the lion away and kill him if we can." Several of the villagers were brave enough to follow Mankwala. But the cowards made excuses for themselves.

"Oh, he'll soon go away by himself!" they jeered. "It's useless to go searching for a lion."

The brave ones started out. Mankwala led the way, a razor-sharp spear in his strong hands. Suddenly the ground rocked with a terrific roar, and the gigantic lion leaped upon Mankwala and threw him to the ground.

All the other men ran away or climbed trees nearby, but one half-grown boy took pity on Mankwala caught in the clutches of the vicious beast. Suddenly Mankwala sat up and plunged his spear deep into the beast's flanks. At the same minute, the boy rushed in and plunged his spear into the lion's neck.

With an agonized roar, the lion dropped Mankwala and sprang onto the boy. Then with one last howl he fell over dead. The frightened men crept down out of the trees now and made three litters. One was for Mankwala, one was for the boy, and one was for the dead lion with the two spears sticking into him.

Poor Mankwala was so badly mauled that he passed away that same night, but he was a Christian, and he died with a prayer on his lips. They carried the boy to the nearest mission hospital, where he had to stay for several months. When he got out, he changed his name.

"My name now is Mkute wa Mkango," he said. When people called him this new name, they would remember every time they said it that he was only a "fragment of lion's flesh."

Master Sidwala was away at another school when the messengers came to tell him that the lion had killed his uncle. Poor Mankwala had been in his grave for several days when Master got back to his village to see the place where they had laid him. As he stood by the rough grave, his heart was heavy with great sorrow. Here lay one of the best friends he ever had. Here lay the one who had led him out of idolatry into the happy light of Christianity. And he began to weep there by his uncle's grave.

Master had learned many things at his new school. He had learned that Saturday, not Sunday, is the Sabbath. He had learned that the dead sleep quietly in their graves until the resurrection. But he had learned one even more important thing, something which made him sure that his uncle would inherit eternal life. He had learned that God judges men by what they know, and how they have used the knowledge they have.

Even in his sorrow, Master felt great joy filling his heart. "Mankwala will have eternal life! God will be merciful to Mankwala because he lived a good life," he said.

Master Sidwala became an important man at Malamulo Mission. He took correspondence courses and learned enough to become head bookkeeper and accountant for the Malamulo Press. He and Fales, his wife, are teaching their children to be Christians, too.

On Sabbath Master sits at one end of a backless brick pew at Malamulo church. Fales sits at the other. Flora, Etta, Elmie, and three little boys sit in between. They fill up the whole seat. Sometimes Master tells the children about Uncle Mankwala and about their "adversary the devil," who goes about "as a roaring lion, . . . seeking whom he may devour."

SOMEONE WHO CARES

*D*EAR LORD, I don't want to quit school! Help me! Oh, please help me find some way to go to college!" The words were hardly audible, and the girl's face was drawn in that anxious, taut attitude of one who asks a favor and fully expects an unfavorable answer.

Esther's faith had had a terrific blow that morning. When she rushed joyously up to her dormitory room from the last-period class, she met the dean distributing the mail.

"A letter for you, Esther." The dean smiled and walked on.

Dad's familiar scrawl was on the envelope, and her heart beat hard with love for him as she tore it open. Then the frightening words jumped out at her from the closely written page: "Mary . . . hemorrhage . . . doctor

154

every day," and Esther, knowing the terrible struggle dad was having to keep her in school, realized that his budget could never encompass it all. Graduation was just four days away, and she had already made her plans to go straight on to college after she graduated. Now she feared those plans would never be carried out.

Esther's faith had shattered in a million fragments. Somehow she managed to smile heroically. She put on her graduation dress, read her speech, and did a thousand other things that she knew she *must* do. Then she went home. College, for the present, seemed as remote as the South Pole.

Eight years passed, during which Esther went to summer school and gulped up in great, indigestible drafts the education courses dispensed there. Then she joined the ranks of elementary school teachers. Come September, Esther found herself in a sunny, cheery schoolroom with twenty children, grades one to four, eyeing her expectantly.

"Cheep! Cheep! Cheep!" suggested a bird in a tree by the window.

"No, I won't be cheap!" she told the bird. And she wasn't. The boys and girls adored their enthusiastic young teacher. But when the church asked her to take the little school again the next year, she blushed and said, "No."

"Why not?" queried the church elder. "Haven't we been good to you?"

"Yes! Yes! But, well—I—I'm going to be married."

When the next autumn came, Esther felt a little lost. September had always meant school of some kind. But she had an idea, which she decided to talk over with her husband.

"Harry, sometime, suppose you and I go to college. I've always wanted to do that."

Harry rubbed his smooth face dry with the towel before he answered. Then he came over and pulled a chair close to hers.

"Why, Esther, that's been a pet ambition of mine, too. I've always thought I'd like to study Greek, ancient history, and theology. Let's work toward that."

Before long the pennies began to clatter into a fruit jar labeled "College Fund." Harry continued to work full time until the depression struck the entire country.

Then little handfuls of coins had to be fished out of the fruit jar to pay for a quart of milk or a loaf of bread or a pound of rice, and hope gradually evaporated. Harry worked spasmodically, whenever he could find work to do, and the wolf cast his shadow perilously near their door many times.

By the time little Johnny was six and Raymond four, you would think that Esther and Harry would have forgotten all about college. Work was more plentiful, but at the same time their desire to learn had taken a new trend.

Every night after Johnny and Ray were snug in their beds, Esther cleaned the kitchen table. A lesson from the Home Study Institute was spread out, leaves of books fluttered, and pens scratched on examination sheets.

One day, possessed by a sudden inspiration, Esther wrote to a nearby college. She told them what kind of work

Harry did and suggested that if they ever needed help in that line, she and Harry were available. There was a courteous, disinterested reply in a few days, then nothing. But Esther and Harry never stopped praying.

In the middle of April, a year later, a letter came addressed to Mr. Harry Benning.

"We are wondering," read the letter, "if you are still interested in going to college. We need a man with your experience. If you can come, kindly write us immediately."

"Interested!" repeated Harry, as he read the letter.

"Interested!" echoed Esther, starry-eyed.

The next September, Johnny and Ray trotted off to the elementary school, and Esther and Harry enrolled as college freshmen. Esther chose an English major, and how she enjoyed her themes, reports, and debates! Harry, meanwhile, was deeply engrossed in his long-anticipated study, theology.

It was not easy going, but God looked after Harry and Esther. When they needed something, somehow, miraculously, it was there.

One day Harry remarked, "Esther, did you notice that my shirts are wearing out?"

"Yes, I did, dear. We'll have to pray for more. God knows you need shirts."

"Yes, we need to have more faith! God is good to us, Esther," Harry declared as he started out the door on his way to work.

Esther was washing the breakfast dishes when she heard a knock at the door. She opened it to greet one of her neighbors. Mrs. Brown, a widow, stood on the front step, smiling apologetically.

"I hope you won't be offended, Mrs. Benning," she began, "but I brought your husband some shirts. You know the people I work for are very wealthy, and they gave them to me. They've scarcely been worn." And she unwrapped four beautiful shirts.

"While we are yet speaking, He will answer," thought Esther. Aloud she said, "Why, Mrs. Brown, we were just praying for shirts." And the two women looked at each other understandingly.

"Have you learned that, too?" asked the good old woman. "I've had to lean hard on the Lord since my husband died." And the tears stood in her faded blue eyes.

Esther and Harry finished college, and many times during those four hard, exciting years they felt the closeness of the heavenly Father.

"I'm going to appreciate these years," remarked Harry. "I've learned a lot—in school, and out."

"I've learned that the Lord really cares if we're low on food or need a pair of shoes!" added Esther. "I know He's been with us every bit of the way."

THE DOG
THAT INTERRUPTED
THE PREACHER

*A*FTER Maccabees died, we didn't think we could ever love another pet. We were sure that Maccabees was the most adorable kitten in the world. She was yellow and white, with blue eyes and a white throat and the most innocent little face you ever saw.

Our son Charles was deeply engrossed in reading the Apocrypha at the time we got her, so he dubbed her Maccabees, and she grew to know her name very well.

When autumn came, a few mice got into the house. Little Maccabees prepared herself for battle, and soon the mice disappeared. Sometimes she'd run to me, mewing, and I knew she wanted help. If the mouse had taken refuge under the piano, grandpa's cane would rout it, and Maccabees could pounce on it. If it had hidden behind some boxes in the closet, I must move them. Maccabees knew I'd help her.

She learned to sit up like a dog, walk on her hind legs, and even climb the door, peep in the window, and mew whenever she wanted in. The whole family babied her unbelievably.

Arlene, the girl who lived next door, used to come over every night to play with her; so when Maccabees heard the familiar crunch of her footsteps on the walk after supper, she would run to the door and mew for someone to let Arlene in.

One night after supper, Charles had to go back to school for a meeting. He left happy, but in five minutes he was back, the tears streaming down his cheeks. He was carrying the battered, tiny body of little Maccabees. She had decided to follow him to the school. In her effort to catch up with his long strides, she had run right in front of an automobile.

"Mother," Charles sobbed, "Maccabees is done for! She's dead, Mother!"

I cried, too. So did my husband and Arlene. We put the little body into a shoe box and covered it with a piece of pink silk from my scrap basket. We buried Maccabees out in our backyard near a rosebush.

The next day I had to drive to Minneapolis on business. Just as I was backing out of the garage, my husband came out to the car. "See if you can find some kind of pet for Charles while you're in the city," he whispered. "Look in the newspaper. Every day there are ads about people who want to give their pets away. Bring him something."

I agreed, even though it was right in the middle of the depression and we certainly didn't have the money to buy a pet.

As I approached the outskirts of the city, I happened to notice a sign for the city dog pound. On an impulse, I parked and went in.

In cages around the rooms a hundred different dogs barked, snarled, whined, and howled. An old man showed me around after informing me I could have my pick of the lot for two dollars.

It was hard to decide! I looked carefully at a pretty black cocker spaniel, even more carefully at a beautiful Scotch collie that cried and begged me to take him.

But ours was not a large house; therefore I had to choose a small dog. The old man led me to a cage containing a tiny toy terrier that greeted me like a long-lost friend. He was black and white with a funny little tail that curled once, then started around again. I knew he was the dog for me.

When I got him home, Charlie—who by now was reading *Otto von Bismarck*—decided to call that little scrap of a dog Otto von Bismarck. We shortened it, of course, to Otto.

Our home was never the same again! Though we never quite forgot Maccabees, little Otto took her place with all the enthusiasm he could muster, and he mustered a lot. Soon he was learning faster than many children I know.

First, he learned to sit up on his hind legs; but to this

11

he added a trick of his own. He'd thrash the air with his
front paws as if he were saying something very important.
He did this particularly well after he had learned where
the candy jar was!

Next we taught him to catch the candy in his mouth
and bark "Thank you."

When our boys went off to college, Otto stayed at home
with us. I continued to teach him tricks so that when the
boys came home he could show off. He loved to do that!

When the boys would breeze in the door, the first
thing they'd say would be, "Got any cake or cookies?" The
second thing would be, "Does Otto know any new tricks?"

"Otto," I'd say, "go practice your music lesson." He
would trot straight to the piano bench and sit up on it, just
the right distance from the keys. He had to have a piece of
music or a hymnbook in front of him so that he could stop
and smell it significantly, on occasion. Then, in between
his sniffings, his furry paws would play a merry tune all
over the keys. The boys laughed at him till they were
breathless. I always rewarded him for every concert with a
piece of his favorite candy—cone-shaped chocolate creams.

In addition to his musical talents, Otto could jump
through a hoop, over a stick, and could carry a basket. But
I taught him one trick that I wish I hadn't because it got
me into trouble.

I would bend over and pat my back and say, "Jump
up." Otto would get a running start and jump right up on
my back. That was all right when I was prepared and
wanted him up there; but it got so I couldn't pick up a

pin or lean over to straighten a rug, or even bend over to get a kettle out of the cupboard, without getting Otto on my back. I would have to look around warily every time I needed to bend down for something to be sure that no little dog was backing up getting ready to leap.

One day while I was shopping in town, I noticed a poor old woman hobbling along ahead of me. She dropped a small package and bent over to get it. Instantly Otto was up on her poor old back, and she was screaming pitifully. Quickly I pulled him off, explaining that he was only a little trickster and meant no harm. I rubbed her back while Otto ran all around us in a spasm of delight, as if he had really accomplished something. Pretty soon the woman was laughing and said the whole thing brightened her day.

I thought, ruefully, that life with Otto was just a little too full of adventure. We continued our shopping, and I told Otto to stay right beside me. He had a habit of running off to beg scraps at the butcher shop, and I was afraid he'd get run over and killed.

Suddenly I turned around and saw the little dog sneaking out the store door. A huge fat man was right in front of him, and Otto had taken advantage of his opening the door. "Otto, come right back here," I said sternly. To my chagrin, man and dog both paused in the doorway and then turned around and came back toward me.

"Vot? Did you call me, missus? I heard vunce dot you say Otto."

It was my turn to blush. "I was just calling my dog," I said. "His name is Otto."

"Vell, so am I Otto!" he replied, and everyone in the store had a good laugh at our expense.

I started teaching church school that fall, and Otto entered into another phase of his career. He just did not understand why he couldn't attend school. He came at recess and became a fielder for the ball game that was always in lively progress in the backyard. When the bell rang, he would get into line with the boys and girls, and my heart of stone would nearly melt, but I always made him go home. I knew if he came in, no one would study. "No, Otto," I would say. "You can't come to school. Now go home." His curly tail would uncurl and droop between his legs. He'd crawl almost on his stomach, pleading with me. But school was business, and I'd say, "No, no," and close the door right in his cute little face. Otto had a forgiving heart, though. He'd be at the school door every night, ready to accompany me home.

Once Arthur White came to speak at the academy. He told many of the fascinating experiences of his grandmother, Ellen G. White. He had the big Bible with him which his grandmother held while she was in vision.

Since all his meetings were at night, I knew that some of my church school children wouldn't get to hear him. I begged him to come and talk at the school.

"When may I come?" he asked.

"Anytime," I told him eagerly. "Just anytime. Nothing is more important than building the children's faith. We'll lay down any lesson we may be studying."

It was so peaceful the day he came. The schoolhouse

was clean and orderly. Indian summer breezes lifted the snowy curtains. An old cow belonging to one of the neighbors had wandered into the schoolyard and was munching on the grass.

I didn't know, however, that Yvonne, one of my mischievous ten-year-olds, had finally given in to Otto's pleading that day. She had carried him inside carefully concealed in her red coat. In the bustle of getting seated, she transferred the tiny little fellow to a paper box in the corner. He knew he wasn't supposed to be there and was keeping very, very quiet so I wouldn't find out. He curled up and went right to sleep, and all would have been well if—— Well, that's something else again.

Pastor White began telling stories of the early days of the church. He told of tiring journeys, when Elder and Mrs. James White sat up in a carriage all night long in order to get to the next meeting. Then he launched into an exciting story of their trip by boat down the Mississippi River.

"They were riding a big side-wheeler," he said. "Often, to amuse themselves during the long trip, they leaned over the side and watched the other river traffic. The river was crowded in those days because there were no good roads leading south. Mrs. White noticed barges floating along, full of lumber from the North Woods. The men sitting on the barges called up to them, 'Got anything to read?' "

Then Pastor White, in order to make the story more real to the wide-eyed children, added a few sound effects. We could almost hear the chug, chug of the engine

and the splash, splash of the paddle wheels. We imagined
we could almost see Elder and Mrs. White leaning over
talking to the news-hungry lumberjacks. But Otto heard
those sound effects, too. The children were leaning for-
ward in their seats, living the story themselves. Suddenly
Otto jumped out of his box, the hair on his back standing
straight up, and charged at the man who was making all
those whirring and chugging sounds.

Pastor White retreated hastily. I would have, too, if I
hadn't known that Otto would never attack a preacher in-
tentionally. I jumped up immediately and put the little
troublemaker outside, where he belonged.

Then Pastor White continued the story. He told how
James White tied pieces of coal to copies of the *Review*
and *Present Truth* and tossed them down to the eager
men on the barges. "We'll never know till the judgment
day just what things like that have accomplished," he said.

Pastor White seemed to have a never-ending supply of
interesting stories. "Now our little dog here reminds me of
a lovely black Jersey heifer my grandmother had. It was a
beautiful animal, and Mrs. White loved it dearly.

"When the hired man went to milk her, grandmother
would sometimes go along. She'd pat the cow's silky coat.
The pretty animal loved her and would always answer
her gentle talk in soft moos. 'Co, co, bossy,' she'd say.
'Moo, moo-o-o, moo-o,' the cow would answer, and would
rub her silky head against grandmother's arm."

That sound effect was too much for the gentle bossy in
the schoolyard. Suddenly, right in the midst of Pastor

White's mooing, my curtains were thrust aside, and the shiny nose of the neighbor's cow entered the conversation. "Moo-oo, moo-oo," she answered Pastor White.

We laughed till we were weak. Pastor White assured me he would never forget our school!

Poor little Otto ran afoul of a vicious billy goat during one of his excursions around town. The rough old goat must have given Otto an exceedingly bad time, for ever afterward when he came to that place, he would make a wide detour and go by on the other side of the street. Even the word *goat* in ordinary conversation would raise his hair and set off a low, angry growl deep down in his throat.

Soon after that my husband and I went as missionaries to Central Africa. We left Otto with our son's wife's parents, the Sansonettis. He captured their hearts, too; but I missed the little dog. I wondered if he'd remember me when I came home after seven long years. I think he did. He walked in circles around me, his face a mask of confusion. I slept at the Sansonettis', and the next morning I was awakened by Otto's cold little nose nudging my hand. Suddenly I thought of the goats! I knew he had not seen any goats around Chicago. If he'd remember goats, I was sure he'd remember me. I sat up. "Otto," I said, "are there goats out there?" Instantly, he was at the window, looking out at the swirling traffic, his hair standing on end, barking at the goats he'd seen seven years before.

Otto is dead now, but our whole family remembers him as a bright spot in our lives.

LUWAZI— OR BUST!

I'LL NEVER forget the night we almost didn't reach Luwazi. Luwazi is a mission station in Africa, about eight hundred miles below the equator. That morning we packed our things in two jeep station wagons. We planned to drive the five hundred miles to Luwazi to hold some meetings. I rode in one car with Pastor and Mrs. Webster while my husband went with Pastor Pierce in the other. The skies were blue, the air was pure and fresh, and our courage was at an all-time high.

At noon we stopped by the side of the road to eat lunch. We drank some of the water we carried. Everyone takes his water with him in Africa, or regrets it later. The water wasn't cold, but we had learned to enjoy it because it was wet and be glad we had some, regardless of the

168

temperature or the flavor. Mrs. Webster uncovered a big dish of crusty baked beans, which we scooped into little dishes and ate with our sandwiches. A big banana apiece was our dessert.

We stopped at a little village and found a mud house with a grass roof and a rough floor where we could sleep. We fixed our food in a tiny grass kitchen outside over an open fire. Villagers brought us a bucket of milk, and someone else brought a basket of lemons, some onions, and a basket of potatoes not much bigger than marbles. The beds were rough and uncomfortable. During the night I heard a lion roar in the distance, and a hyena sniffed all around our mud hut, crying out so close that I was sure I could hear him breathe.

We ate a quick breakfast the next morning in order to get an early start. The cars stayed close together so that we could help each other in case we needed it. We were hundreds of miles from any place where we could buy gasoline, and even farther from a mechanic. Naturally, we carried plenty of gasoline with us.

The scenery gradually grew more grand and awesome. Great mountain crags towered above us so high that we looked to see if there was snow on their summits. Green valleys swooped down, thick with elephant grass, bush trees, and kafir corn.

We were happy as we pushed ahead, expecting to get to the mission before the sun went down and Sabbath crept over the hills of central Africa. We were close enough to our destination that we decided not to stay with the other car. We would hurry on ahead and get things ready.

The missionaries who lived at Luwazi were away on furlough, and we had sent word ahead for the African helpers to boil water and put a few other things in shape. But we would have to make up beds, put away our clothes, and probably prepare food for the Sabbath after we arrived.

Donato, the cook who worked for the mission family, had sent word that he would be glad to help us with our food while we were there. In our mind's eye we could almost envision the comfort of arriving, dusty and tired, to enjoy a delicious hot supper.

The jeep took a sharp corner just then and suddenly shook all over with a vicious, grinding bang.

"Wow! I didn't see that big rock in the road," muttered Pastor Webster, swerving a bit.

"Think it did any harm?" asked his wife anxiously.

"Oh, no," her husband assured her. "But I'll have to watch more closely after this."

We had gone perhaps two hundred yards when the engine skipped, choked, and died. We got out to see what was wrong. A ribbon of wet stretched behind us. We picked up some red dirt and smelled it. Gasoline! The stone had ripped a hole in our tank, and here we were stranded, miles from a mechanic. It was four o'clock in the afternoon, and we were at least fifteen miles from the mission. "Oh, well," we thought, "we're all right now. The other car will come along in a few minutes, and it can push us in to the mission."

But it didn't come. And it didn't come. And it didn't

come. We were hungry. We were thirsty. We were dirty. We were tired of sitting all crowded up in the jeep.

After it got dark, we didn't dare stay outside the car for fear of wild animals. It was suffocatingly hot inside until we opened the windows. Then mosquitoes feasted on our arms and necks, and we knew we were getting malaria germs by the thousands from their nasty little hypo needles.

Five o'clock. Six. Seven. Where were those men? Eight, nine, ten o'clock. Something terrible must have happened to them. Our tongues were dry, and our skin stung with a million swelling, burning bites. Then we saw a flash of bright light around the corner. The other car was coming! We turned the headlights on and off, signaling. But no. Lightning had made the flash. We knew, because it was followed by such loud thunder in the mountains that we felt as though some clumsy giant had dropped a gigantic bag of mammoth marbles. Instantly another zig-zag incision split the western sky, and we saw the bare crags black and clear against the flaming sky. The thunder was so loud that it shook the ground under us.

The fireworks grew more spectacular around midnight. Longingly we dreamed of a cool bath and a bed with white, smooth sheets to creep between. We dozed a little, and dreamed again of cool drinks, orange juice, papaya juice, cold milk.

"Two o'clock," someone sighed. Then, "Two thirty." Another burst of light. We were sure it was only lightning. We'd been disappointed so many times already. But it wasn't! It was another car. Excited, we scrambled out. We found out that they had had trouble, too—a clogged-up fuel line. But now they could push us. It wouldn't take long to go that last fifteen miles to Luwazi.

Relieved, we got into the car, and the pushing began.

We were making fine time when the downpour hit us. The wheels of the jeep that was pushing spun, and finally couldn't move another inch. We slid clear back to the bottom of one long hill.

Then we had a council of war and decided that the good jeep would take the women on ahead so that we could get things ready. Meanwhile, the men could pull the empty car.

We crept—soaked, muddy, and exhausted—through the streaming rain to the other jeep. The mud slogged in our shoes, while streams of drenching rain ran down our backs. We huddled in the car, dripping and cold, for the windows had to be open so that the driver could see the road. At last the gates of the mission came into view. The car came to a grinding, slithering, mud-slinging stop. It simply couldn't make that last waterlogged hill.

Suddenly, out of the streaming night, Africans appeared all around us. They grabbed the rope which we quickly tied to our bumper, and a hundred or so of them literally dragged us into the mission.

We were in such a daze by now that we hardly realized that we were at our journey's end. Someone had to open the door and tell us to get out. Stiff and weary, we crept up to the mission house. The door opened, and Pastor

Simon Ngaiyaye, one of our pioneer African ministers, stood before us. Behind him we could see a warm fire leaping in the fireplace.

A huge bunch of ripe bananas lay near the hearth. Shaking like wet dogs, we sat down gratefully in front of the blaze. Nothing mattered except that mellow warmth. When the bananas were broken off and passed around, I ate four, even though my hands were crusty with dirt. I never tasted anything so delicious in all my life.

Later, when we had bathed in water that had been carried from the river and heated, we all sat down to breakfast. We were sagging with weariness. But the buttered toast, half a golden-yellow papaya, and the scrambled eggs that Donato cooked for us tasted like ambrosia.

The men and the other jeep arrived in a little while, and we were able to make them comfortable, too. As we fell asleep, we hoped that the next time God gave us a special job to do, He would make the going a little less adventurous.

GOD'S
MYSTERIOUS WAYS

*I*T WASN'T fair. Every boy and girl in the church was making excited plans to go to the new academy, except Ben. Ben sat in the back row of the junior Sabbath School class at the Parker Falls church and wished he could run away and get lost.

The new academy was going to be fantastic. The church elder had taken some of the young people down there, some forty-five miles away, to the dedication ceremony. Ben had gone, but he hurt so badly inside that he was sure someone would see his heart bleeding. There was Jim Weaver, right up in the front, asking the conference president where the boys' dormitory was going to be built. Jim ran right to the area and said, "Look, Ben; my room will be right here."

174

Then there was Beth. By the time a boy is in the eighth grade, he gets his eye on some girl he admires more than the rest. And Ben thought Beth was really something special. Beth was going to the academy, too; and she was running all around looking things over, her fair hair getting curlier by the minute.

Then Ben thought of home. There was dad, who loved the bottle a lot more than he loved his family; and mother, who couldn't seem to keep the house clean the way the other boys' mothers did. Ben was ashamed if any of the kids dropped in unexpectedly. He had a paper route and paid his church school tuition himself, so he usually stayed away from the kids outside of school hours. No one knew what was inside Ben's heart. He had locked it up tight with fierce pride.

He had been baptized and had stayed true to the church, even though not another soul in his family gave him a bit of help. He knew he must not eat pork, but ma put pork in everything on the table, till he almost starved to death. Mother knew better, too, for she had been an Adventist once.

Ben would sit sometimes and shake his young head, and then go in and try to bring order out of the snarl ma had left in the kitchen. He had washed many a sinkful of dishes and put a couple of potatoes in the oven to bake so as to have some food without the pork flavoring.

Of course, Ben's mother had never been to church school. Ben had learned much about the good life since he started going to church school.

In his daily Bible lessons he learned about the prophecies, of "wars and rumours of wars," and famines, and all that. In history class he found out that time was in the toes of the great image of Daniel 2. That meant that the old earth was on the home stretch now, and there was no use wasting a lot of time on foolishness, when the end was so close.

But church school was almost over, and Ben could not sell enough papers to pay his tuition at the academy. That was as impossible as flying to the moon, he thought. He could never do it.

There were probably some kind people who, if they had known how badly Ben wanted to go, might have helped him. But Ben would die before he'd ask for help. Besides, there was a great depression going on then, and most folks had to dig for what they had. There was little left to help anyone else.

So Beth and the others went to the beautiful new academy. Letters came home about the fun they were having. They talked about the marches on Saturday nights and Friday night vespers, with the organ playing "Day Is Dying in the West" and everyone wearing his best clothes, and the halls polished till they looked like glass.

Beth told him that they always had sandwiches on Friday night. "They have the best sandwiches you ever tasted, Ben," she had written. "I'll make you some when I come home. They're called Egg Savory. I could eat a dozen if I wasn't afraid I'd start saying, 'Oink, oink.' " That sounded just like Beth.

Gradually, Ben became an outsider as far as the old group was concerned. He got work with a company in town. He learned bookkeeping and accounting, and he had Sabbaths off. He taught himself to type, and then got a shorthand book and worked on that. But he allowed his heart to grow bitter as gall. "Why? Why? Why?" he asked again and again. Why was he shut out when all the others were allowed into that magic world at the academy. Finally he quit going to church.

There was one thing, though, that he never did. He never worked on the Sabbath. His bosses were so pleased with the excellent work he did that they never asked him anything about his religion. They just went on letting him off on Friday at four o'clock, and he never had to go to work on the Sabbath.

His mother asked him a time or two why he had quit going to church, but he didn't want to talk about it.

"Oh, I just quit going," he told her.

"Don't you think it's the right church anymore?" she asked, eyeing him sharply.

"Oh, yes, Mother, it's right," he said, a bit too fiercely. And he grabbed his hat and started to leave.

"Well, don't bite my head off. You're just sore because you can't go to that academy," she answered. "If your father had any 'get-up-and-go' about him, you could have gone with Beth and the rest. But, no, we don't get anything around here. The saloons get it all. They——"

Ben ran out the door then, for he didn't want to hear the long list of his mother's grievances.

12

By the time his old group graduated from academy, Ben had $600 saved up. If he couldn't have an education, he would have a fine home, he decided, something that he need not be ashamed of the rest of his life. He worked hard and saved every cent he could scrape together. He helped ma, of course; but he saved every bit he could after that.

Then one day he met a beautiful girl. She came into the office with her father on some business, and Ben completely lost his head. Before long they were married, but there was one thing Ben could not bring himself to tell her—that he could not work on Sabbath. And he could not go to the store or work around the house either.

It was embarrassing, sometimes, the fixes he would get into. Jeanie, his wife, would say early on Saturday mornings, "Ben, this would be a good day to mow the lawn," or "Ben, could you run to the store and get me a dozen eggs?"

It was amazing how he got out of such predicaments all the time, but he did. He usually left early in the morning and went to the library. He hardly knew why he was so strict with himself, unless it was something that old Brother Cunningham used to talk about at prayer meeting sometimes. It was called the unpardonable sin.

"What is the unpardonable sin, Brother Cunningham?" he had asked timidly.

"It's a terrible, terrible thing, Ben," good old Brother Cunningham had said. "You know how tough the soles of your feet get when you run barefoot all summer? You can run over sharp stones, and they don't hurt you. Right?"

"Oh, yes," Ben had said and laughed. "But when you first get your shoes off in the spring, your feet sure are tender!"

"Well, that's the way with our consciences and sin, Ben," the kind old man had explained. "When we first come into the family of God, we're all tender, and every sin hurts like crazy. The thing to do is to stay away from sin, so we don't get all toughened up and it doesn't seem like sin anymore."

Ben thought of Bert, who used to go to church. Now he smoked and ate pork and worked on the Sabbath. He remembered Isabel, who had wanted to be a missionary. Now she went to dances all the time, and she looked cheap and almost second-class somehow. He did not want to get tough like Isabel or Bert. He didn't want to commit that unpardonable sin.

Jeanie would tell her friends, "My husband is the strangest eater you ever saw. He won't eat pork or drink coffee or even a Coke. I never saw the beat of it. Just set him down to a plate of plain cornbread and beans, and he thinks he's having a feast."

"Well, you're lucky," her friends would tell her. "My husband has to have all kinds of fancy food and wants a big meal every night. I get so tired I could die, just hanging over the stove all day."

Jeanie would laugh. "I have it easy, I'll tell you. He'd just as soon have bread and milk as anything. I guess I ought to be glad."

Ben never told Jeanie, or anyone else, the thoughts

that plagued his mind every day. He heard that Jim was studying to be a nurse, and that Carla had gone to college, and so had Beth. He didn't feel bad anymore; he just felt dully interested in what the old gang were doing. Then Beth got married to a young minister. Still Ben didn't tell Jeanie about the church, though he thought about it often on the Sabbaths when he went to the park or the library. Jeanie thought sometimes he was at work, but actually he never lifted his hand to break the Sabbath.

Then Jeanie begged him to learn how to play a new game that her friends and their husbands played. He refused at first, but she was so sweet, and she sat down beside him with the deck and showed him how easy it was and how much fun. The first thing he knew, he was playing it with his wife—and beating her, to her delight.

"Why, Ben, you catch on so quickly! I can't wait to tell the girls. We can have more fun, if you only will, Ben. They all think you are a stuffed shirt and won't have fun with us. But you will, won't you, dear?"

He wouldn't promise, though—not yet. He kept thinking about his church school teacher, who said, "No good ever came from playing cards, boys. And no good ever comes with compromising, either." Ben thought of this now, as he held the innocent-looking cards. Jeanie had told him their names. There was the ace of spades, and cards that had pictures of kings or queens on them, and one called the joker. Yet, he reasoned quietly to himself, why was he holding out at all? He wasn't going to church. It had been years since he had seen much of the old crowd he used to love. He had let bitterness and frustration separate him from them. Finally, Jeanie begged and begged until he consented to have a card party at their house. It would be the next Saturday night.

"You'll just have to help me today, if you can get off," Jeanie said. Ben stood and looked at her. It was a lovely Sabbath morning. Across town Sabbath School was beginning. Funny he should remember that, after all these years. Off in another state, Beth's husband was a minister at a big church. Carla was a missionary in Africa. Jim was a nurse in a big sanitarium near Columbus, Ohio. And he, Ben, who had been in the very same church school, under the very same teachers, was getting ready for a silly card game.

Suddenly Ben felt reckless. It was no use. He got the hose and hooked it up and began to wash the car. Later he cleaned out the garage and trimmed the hedge and shook the rugs, and had time to run to the supermarket. Pretty soon, he saw the sun going down on the Sabbath he had not kept. Oh, why did he feel so sick inside?

"Well, we surely got a lot done today, Ben," Jeanie said happily. She had the card tables set up in the pretty living room. On the buffet were plates of delicious sandwiches and cookies of all kinds, fresh from Jeanie's oven. The percolator was bubbling on the stove. Jeanie was old-fashioned enough to like her coffee a certain way.

In just a little while the house was full of people. They were going around with coffee cups and plates with sandwiches, laughing and talking. Ben stood back and watched them. This was the Sabbath he had not kept. Now he was at his first card party. Jeanie was triumphant that she had finally gotten her quiet husband into the swing of things. She laughed and seemed as happy as a lark. Eventually they got settled down at the tables for some serious card playing.

They had been playing only about ten minutes when Jeanie said, "It's your turn, Ben." But he did not move. Suddenly he lurched and fell from the chair. The merry party was suddenly all confusion. One of the women straightened up the house while Jeanie went to the hospital in the ambulance with her unconscious husband. No one knew just what had happened. Could it have been a heart attack? Ben was too young to have a stroke. But it was surely something serious. He was unconscious most of the night.

Toward morning he began to regain consciousness. He hardly knew where he was at first. His poor mother was weeping by his bed, trying to smooth the bedclothes and the pillow. His father, sober for once, looked very serious. But by his side was dear Jeanie, the coolest one of them all, ready to tell him where he was, and to piece together the happenings in his confused mind. He said little until his father and mother were gone and he was alone with Jeanie.

He turned on his side and took her hand.

"I know what's the matter with me, Jeanie," he said quietly. "And I want you to listen and not interrupt me or think I'm crazy till I'm through. I have made a mistake in not telling you a lot of things long ago. I should have, for I believe what I'm going to tell you, and I love you so much that I should have let you know."

Then Ben told her about church school and the Sabbath. He told her the Bible verses he remembered all those years that proved that the Sabbath is the seventh day.

"You've probably wondered why I was gone every Saturday, Jeanie, why I wouldn't go to the store for you. Well, I couldn't bring myself to it. I was jealous and hurt. I felt the Lord was unfair because He didn't give me the same breaks the other kids in school had. I was bitter, but I knew it was the truth, so I could never bring myself to give it up entirely. I didn't want to commit the unpardonable sin."

Jeanie smoothed his brown hair and smiled. "You should have told me, dear. I would have understood."

"Well, last Sabbath—yesterday—I broke the Sabbath, the first time. Do you remember? Then we had that card party. There were all kinds of things there that I have been taught are wrong. People were smoking, and you know how Hank poured a little whiskey in his coffee and said he was making it good the way his old Irish grandpa liked it. And the cards, Jeanie."

"Dear, I didn't know you felt so strongly about it," Jeanie protested again.

"But that wasn't the worst thing, Jeanie. While I held those cards in my hand, suddenly I looked down, and there right by my chair was a horrible deep pit. I could see you all laughing and talking, but my chair was slowly crumbling over the side of that pit. I tried to scream, I tried to catch myself, but, Jeanie, I began to fall into that terrible hole. I never felt such a horrible sensation in all my life. I thought I was lost forever.

"Suddenly I looked up, and right on the edge of the pit was the loveliest Being I ever saw. Jeanie, I know it was Jesus. He reached down and took me by the hand and pulled me up. I never felt such joy in all my life. He said only four words, and I know I'll never forget them.

" 'I need you, Ben,' was what He said. And, Jeanie, I must follow Him. I hope you'll go with me, for I must follow Him all the way."

"I will, Ben. I will go with you, and with Him—all the way."

That next Friday night, Jeanie and Ben started going to church. And though that was more than thirty years ago, they have been going all the way with Jesus ever since. Ben is the elder of the church now, and if you should visit their church, Ben and Jeanie would probably ask you to go home with them to dinner. Ben might even show you where the deep pit was right in his dining room, where he caught a fleeting glimpse of how lovely Jesus is. A look will come into his face when he tells it, and you'll know that he can hardly wait to see Jesus and join the family of heaven.

THE FAMILY
OF HEAVEN

*T*HE GOOD SHIP plowed her leisurely way through warm waters of the Indian Ocean. The air was extremely hot, and since that particular boat was not blessed with air conditioning, our cabins resembled a turned-on oven. My husband and I, along with hundreds of other passengers, stayed on the upper decks, where we could occasionally detect a faint zephyr that seemed slightly cooler than the still, heavy air. By laying our deck chairs as low as possible, we lived through several suffocating nights.

In the lounge each night a Greek girl who fancied herself quite a virtuoso perpetuated ear-puncturing atrocities on the piano. She played a sort of melody with one finger of the right hand and made up the chords for the left. Bright announcements of a dance were posted on

185

deck. But no one danced. Everyone was too busy trying to keep cool.

One Sunday afternoon I peeped into the lounge and found it empty. I am not a pianist, but I do enjoy playing hymns. My fingers ached for the feel of the keys, and my ears longed to hear the old melodies. So, deciding that I was quite alone, I took my songbook and slipped into the lounge on that hot Sunday afternoon. I opened the piano, noticing as I did how firmly anchored it was to the wall of the lounge. I know from experience that furniture slides all over the place when the sea is rough. It might be serious if a piano took to pursuing you about the room in the Bay of Biscay.

I opened my book cautiously and began to play. Then I got so interested in an old favorite "game" of mine—starting at the beginning of the hymnbook and seeing how far I can play at one sitting—that I did not notice what was happening. When I looked up, my heart plunged. The lounge was packed with people. They were listening to every song with evident pleasure.

Then they began to call out requests. I was glad then that I had learned to play dozens of hymns from memory when I was a child.

"Can you play 'When I Survey the Wondrous Cross'?" I could, and did.

" 'The Old Rugged Cross'?"

" 'The Touch of His Hand on Mine'?"

" 'The Way of the Cross Leads Home'?"

So it went all that sultry Sunday afternoon. Catholic,

Lutheran, Dutch Reformed, Moravian, Methodist, Baptist, Hindu, and Mohammedan—all listened together. The non-Christians pressed close to the piano so that they could read the words off the book and sing the songs that the rest of us knew by heart.

When I got up, someone handed me a note asking me to go to a certain cabin. When I got there, I found an Anglican vicar of the church, and his wife. He had been very ill with malaria and had been confined to his cabin for several days.

"After days of the unholy uproar of those badly executed dance tunes, your hour of music seemed like a message from another world. Do it again, please."

Later, as I left his cabin for the coolness of the deck, I thought that one need not be ashamed. Jesus is always beautiful.

A few days later I had gathered a group of little children together for a story hour. Two were from Germany, one was from Portugal, and several were from England. Two little Italians were traveling toward Genoa, and there were several others. The way they hung onto my words and edged close to watch every expression on my face made me know that little people of all lands love big people who love them.

The boat stopped one day in Dar es Salaam, a port in Tanganyika (now Tanzania). Trunks were piled up, and our deck steward said that many passengers would be boarding there. I saw one whom I knew must be a missionary. She was a kind, sweet-faced Englishwoman. She

turned and went over to the rail and began to talk to some
African people gathered there to tell her good-bye.

Her face was so full of love and kindness that I moved
closer to watch. Kindness is a rare quality, especially when
one is dealing with the primitive, the ignorant, and the
downtrodden. The people stood there, ragged and poor,
looking up at the face of their missionary, who loved them
and had given years of her life to help them. The tears ran
down their unhappy faces, for they well knew that love
and tolerance like this would be hard to replace.

I do not know what church she represented, but she
displayed such a sweetness of character that it seemed
unimportant. I knew at a glance that day that she was in
close touch with the Source of universal love.

Yes, the Lord has other sheep. I have seen many of
them who know and follow the voice of the Shepherd.

My husband and I had noticed the tall good-looking
doctor from Pakistan several times. He, too, had boarded at
Dar es Salaam. We had smiled and exchanged greetings
with him as we walked on the deck.

One bright evening, when the whole sky seemed to
glow with an unearthly beauty, we stood on the western
side of the boat watching the indescribable sunset. Over
on the other side several devout Mohammedans had their
prayer rugs out and were kneeling toward Mecca.

Dr. Minhas, the Pakistani physician, walked toward
us, looking very agitated. We turned and greeted him
kindly.

"What a difference there is in you Europeans!" he

exclaimed. "Some of you act as if you love everyone, regardless of race. Others——" He spread his hands and
looked across the darkening water, sadness mellowing his
deep-set eyes.

"What's the matter, Doctor?" asked my husband. "Has
something happened to hurt your feelings?"

"Oh"—he tried to laugh—"it is really nothing, I guess,
for one should rise above small hurts. But we are so hu-
man. Slights and insults do hurt. Just now I was coming
out of the lounge, and I walked past that small boy. He
gave me a violent push and said, 'Get out of my way, you
dirty Indian!' "

Looking toward the small child staring impudently at
us, I thought of how cheated he had been in his upbring-
ing. He had never learned how much fun it is to be nice
to people. We had noticed the whole family almost as soon
as they came on board. They were slovenly, ill-bred, with
abominable table manners. Yet they felt superior to a
man who had associated with kings and had climbed to
the top of a fine profession.

We stood there in the dim evening and talked sooth-
ingly with the doctor. I was proud that I was a follower of
One who mingled freely with people His own nation de-
spised, One who discarded the bigoted Pharisaic customs,
even though He died for doing so.

We told our friend that not all Europeans were as
uncouth as the people he had met.

Then he said a surprising thing: "When Jesus comes,
all the wrongs will be made right and all evil will be cov-

ered with His great goodness. I have read that He loved
Jew and Gentile, bond and free, black and white."

Our eyes popped wide open. "Why, do you know, Dr.
Minhas, that Jesus is coming soon?"

He smiled. "Yes, I know," he said happily, "and I
long for His coming. My little boy had a birth injury and
will never walk. My old father is very sick. When Jesus
comes, my little boy will run and play; my old father will
be young again. There will be no more hate, no more race
prejudice."

"Then we shall all sit down together in the kingdom
of our Father," my husband added. "We will all be one
with Him."

A few days after that incident we entered the Red Sea.
The weather was hotter than any I had ever experienced.
We seemed to occupy every hour of the day just trying to
keep cool. I got up early one morning and carried a bundle
of ironing to the laundry room. The sweat was simply
pouring as I hurried to finish my chores before the real
heat set in. The day before, it had been 130 degrees in
some parts of the boat.

Suddenly the whole doorway seemed to be filled with
the gigantic figure of Dr. Minhas.

"Mrs. Edwards!" he exclaimed. "Are you ironing?
You? Why, you must not! You are too dainty, too delicate!"

I giggled inwardly, remembering the meals I had
served, working my way through high school, the floors I
had scrubbed on my hands and knees, and the washings
and ironings I had done to get through college.

He couldn't see my thoughts, however, for he came in masterfully, took the iron, and eased me out of the blistering hot room.

"Go!" he cried. "Go quickly up on the deck before you faint."

I escaped to the upper deck, pondering on King Arthur and the days of chivalry. I knew then that the history books are all wrong. A few knights are still abroad on this earth.

Just outside of our ports of call, I was watching some near-naked stevedores staggering under the weight of great bundles of sisal. A rascally overseer kept up a constant stream of shouting, yelling, and harsh abuse. The poor men were working so hard and they looked so cowed, so forlorn and poor and friendless, that I could hardly keep from crying for them. I wished I could tell them about Jesus, to whom color of skin or poverty or nation made no difference. Then I felt a hand on my shoulder. I turned and looked into the face of a tall sister, dressed in the distinctive habit of her religious order.

"You love these poor people, don't you?" she whispered to me.

I nodded, but I couldn't speak.

"I can tell that it hurts you to see them ill-treated," she said.

Looking at her retreating black-robed figure, I realized again that our Master has other sheep who will one day be in His fold!

An Indian boy, terribly crippled from polio, was with

us often on that voyage. He was lonely, and he seemed to enjoy talking with us. We liked him and listened to his eager descriptions of his home and mother. We in turn answered his naïve questions about "fabulous America." It seemed so little, just taking time to be kind to a lonely Indian lad. It must have helped him, though, for later we got a letter from his father in India.

He wrote: "I am very much indebted to you for the assistance and guidance given to my son, Ved Bhushan Bhardwaj, during voyage period. I am proud my son has given me opportunity for acquaintance with you. A gift parcel containing one beautiful sari has been sent to you. With kindest regards,

"Yours sincerely,
"Jai Dev Bhardwaj"

Halfway around the world a worried father had been warmed and relieved to learn that someone had been kind to his son. I'm glad he knows that we follow Christ. The family of heaven knows no boundaries, and I have learned to treasure those precious other sheep who are often nearer to the kingdom of heaven than we realize.

TEACH Services, Inc.
P U B L I S H I N G

We invite you to view the complete
selection of titles we publish at:
www.TEACHServices.com

We encourage you to write us
with your thoughts about this,
or any other book we publish at:
info@TEACHServices.com

TEACH Services' titles may be purchased in
bulk quantities for educational, fund-raising,
business, or promotional use.
bulksales@TEACHServices.com

Finally, if you are interested in seeing
your own book in print, please contact us at:
publishing@TEACHServices.com

We are happy to review your manuscript at no charge.